DON'T GO
TO THE W
TODAY....

A BISHOP FARTHING/KEN JONES STORY

by Paul Cosway

The Devil's most devilish when respectable.

Elizabeth Barrett Browning 1806 - 61

1

Southampton Airport.

Doina hurries to keep up with her male escort - heart beating wildly, eyes everywhere, taking in all the details she could of the country she hopes will be her new home. She rushes through the terminal, pulling her new carry-on case (all the luggage they'd allowed her to bring) behind her, glimpsing a grey sky through the windows and the distant shapes of green trees. Beyond, the traffic rushing past on the motorway.

The instructions were clear. She had to remain silent, say nothing, pretend no understanding of English. Andrei would do all the talking. He strides confidently, two passports clutched tightly in his right hand. His is genuine. Hers a clever forgery, her surname changed to match his. Clever enough she hopes. She must act the part of a sweet and blushing bride. His story will be that this is their honeymoon. But once in the country, she will be taken to her new job with a wealthy English family and her 'husband' will be gone.

Passport control. The officer looks grim and professional. Her heart skips a beat as he checks their documents and stares hard at her, comparing her face with her picture. It lasts only a second but seems an age. 'How long are you going to stay in this country?' Still the unblinking stare. She opens her mouth, then remembers that she mustn't speak. She closes it again, feeling stupid, looking dumb.

Andrei responds. 'My wife speaks little English. We stay just ten days. It is our honeymoon.'

'You have return tickets?'

Doina's heart thuds. No, she doesn't. She was told she wouldn't need one. But Andrei nods.

'I need to see them.' The officer is suspicious. He looks at Doina. She is only a little over five feet tall: her figure slim and slight. Her hair is long and dark and the eyes, looking timid and nervous, are large and lustrous. Andrei looks at least forty and has an almost arrogant self-confidence. His new bride obviously younger. Very much younger. But Andrei pulls a return ticket from his pocket. It is enough. If he has a return ticket, then obviously his new bride will have one also. The immigrations officer has a long queue to process. He returns their papers and waves them through. 'Congratulations. Enjoy your stay!' She glances back to see how the other couple are faring. They are in a different queue. She gives the girl a little encouraging wave.

Two smartly dressed men in sharp suits wait for passengers to emerge. The two couples are first out, wheeling small carry-on bags. The male passengers look bored and tired. The girls - they don't look much over sixteen - look around excitedly. Doina's eyes sparkle. For them, it's the start of a new life. Without their heavy make-up they would barely pass for fifteen. They're here on the promise of jobs as nannies with rich English families, at salaries astonishing for girls from Eastern Europe.

Unknown to them, their minders' plan is very different. They will be taken to a house of multiple occupancy in the port area of Southampton and gang raped before being put to work servicing the sailors from container ships. Their minders will be brutal: telling them if they refuse, they'll expose them as illegal immigrants and the authorities will throw them into jail.

Their 'husbands' will fly back later to pick up more girls. It's a sleazy trade. But lucrative.

Fifty-two miles away in the rural idyll of North Dorset, Beth finished laying the table for breakfast and then glanced round her country kitchen. It was neat and tidy, with Botanic pattern Portmeirion plates displayed on the dresser and pretty floral curtains at the window. Very different from Peter's austere home, where he works endlessly on his tutoring duties and his research. Last night had been one of their together times and he was slumped in an armchair preparing for an on-line lecture. She pulled Peter from his papers. He still had a couple of hours before work, so there was time for them to do something together before he returned home. She wanted to walk before breakfast – a pleasant stroll down to the nearby woods, where the bluebells, she had heard from Annette, were at their best. Peter unrolls himself from the chair – he is long and lanky with swept back hair that is beginning to grey and makes him look like a mad scientist when the wind catches it. He is painfully shy and it took him months to even say hello to Beth. She is smaller, five feet four, and quiet. She likes music, Laura Ashley country cottage chic and spends hours tending her colourful garden. They have nothing in common.

Together, however, they have found love and companionship. By retaining their own homes and their own individual time and space, they have found a way to keep their romance alive. If this isn't love across the barricades, it is love across an abyss in terms of their tastes and interests. But, as they walk hand in hand down Pinchparson Lane, they are more than content in each other's company.

Their happiness will not last. As they go down to the woods today, they are in for...a very unpleasant surprise.

And the news flies round the village like a bat escaping from hell. A body has been found in Bishop Farthing wood. It lies in a blue sea of wildflowers. It's impossible to see the face. It's as if he'd plunged his mouth into the petals to drink in the pollen. The corpse's fingers are bent and twisted in the bluebell stalks as if to pluck handfuls out of the ground to give to a loved one. But the eyes that stare blindly into the leaf mould thick on the ground will never see a lover again. The twisted limbs will never wrap themselves in an embrace, except with the angel of death.

Peter and Beth are the first to find the body. They stare in horror. Sights such as this are unheard of in this serene setting. Pale and shaking, Peter stabs at the face of his phone, calling emergency services. And Beth screams again and again, as she will in her dreams for years to come.

And for no apparent reason, once the news spreads slowly along the lanes and byways of the string of hamlets that make up the village of Bishop Farthing, many of the villagers find an urgent need to take their dogs for a walk. Trevor, the ex-policeman who had retired to this obscure Dorset village fifteen years before, is the first to stagger down his drive, dragging the unwilling, snarling Fido in tow. His trusty hound has already had two long walks today. Trevor uses these regularly to escape from his home – and his formidable wife – for a couple of hours.

But two walks, thinks Fido, is enough for any dog. He sympathises with his master's need for respite of course, but there is a limit.

Trevor and Fido are just the vanguard of a caravan of good folk who have also decided that a second or third perambulation is just what their dogs need. Several of their canine buddies make their feelings clear, whining in protest as their owners drag them by their leads. One or two dig their nails into the carpet in a futile attempt to be allowed to continue with their nap. But they are picked up and carried, by their determined owners, partway down towards Pinchparson's Bottom, over the old stone bridge by the ford, and along the footpath that crosses the field on the way to the wood.

One by one, a couple of metres between each, the curious neighbours, and their unwilling pooches, saunter through the bluebells, as if totally unaware that anything is amiss. Imagine the feigned looks of surprise on their faces when they see the blue and white police tape that screens the scene of the murder from prying eyes. How strange that so many of them have chosen a route that takes each one as close to the tape as possible.

They can't be blamed for dawdling as they near the scene. After all, it's a long walk down to the wood. They need a break.

2

This was scene that met the gaze of Detective Sergeant Kenneth Jones as he left his car and strode across a field to join his boss at the murder site. Over six feet tall and strongly built, with a good head of auburn hair and clear hazel eyes, he made an impressive sight as he approached the gaggle of onlookers. He wore jeans and a dark blue polo shirt – the day was warm – and designer trainers. By contrast, his superior was shorter, wore a suit and tie (he thought it gave him an air of authority which without it he might have been lacking) and had a face that would have looked bad on a weasel. His grey eyes shifted this way and that. He never looked the person he was talking to straight in the eye. It was a practice that sometimes unnerved suspects and disconcerted everyone else.

Ken had little patience with the nosey parkers who gathered around crime scenes like wasps round a picnic spot. They trampled the ground and threatened forensic evidence. The spectators recognised his authority and parted to let him through. When he ordered them back another fifty yards, they fled without the slightest sign of protest.

He joined Detective Inspector Longbottom and stared with him at the body of a man, lying sprawled across a thorny bramble bush. Ken treated his superior with the courtesy and respect that was appropriate to a senior officer. His year at the training college had taught him this. At times, however, he had to bite his tongue. Longbottom could be slow thinking and lazy. He had spent a lifetime in the force, moving slowly up the ranks - because he was there and the most senior, rather than because he had any real talent for detective work. Ken waited, resignedly, for his superior's first thoughts on the case.

But the Detective Inspector was annoyed, for two reasons. First, the call had summoned him away from what was promising to be a very pleasant afternoon playing golf. Serious crimes were so rare in Dorset that he could usually guarantee a free afternoon most days. Every day.

The second cause for concern was that this could be a murder scene. That could mean days, possibly weeks, maybe months of investigative work. And at the end of all that it might remain unsolved. This would look very bad on his record. And so he was staring at the body, as the police photographer did his work, hoping against hope that this was nothing more than the body of a nature lover who had decided to make his way down to the woods to die.

Another look at his wristwatch. The pathologist was due ten minutes ago. Longbottom cast his professional eye over the corpse and recognised the signs. The way the body lay face down. The angle of the arms, embracing the bluebells. The spread of the legs, neatly avoiding the worst of the brambles. It was clear to the experienced detective that this man had fallen to the ground in a kind of rapture and then had died of natural causes. He made a highly professional decision. Rather than wait any longer, he would have the body turned in order to confirm that there had been no foul play. With any luck he could tie this whole thing up in an hour and still make it to the golf course.

As his assistant returned, the inspector called

to him over the blue and white tape. 'Help me turn this over, sergeant!'

His younger colleague looked first surprised and then uncomfortable. 'Shouldn't we wait for the pathologist, sir?'

'Yes, yes. But there's no need here. No evidence of a crime. Let's just roll him over!'

With great reluctance the sergeant pealed the blue gloves over his hands and then, with a slightly desperate look at the photographer, who reset himself to take pictures of the hidden side of the dead man, he gripped his shoulders and pulled him over.

All eyes went immediately to the chest of the corpse. It was marked with an open wound, surrounded by a huge quantity of blood. The inspector stared in disbelief. After a short, shocked silence, he spoke. 'Bugger!'

His sergeant felt a surge of panic that only got worse as he heard the siren from a 4x4 signalling the arrival of the pathologist. He wasn't sure how she'd react. She didn't suffer fools gladly. He often had to cover for the inspector who, in her opinion, fell into this category. The car stopped in the field as close to the wood as possible and she stepped out. Sergeant Jones felt the usual rush of emotion as her long, elegant form unwound itself and she kicked off her heels and slipped her manicured toes into a pair of trainers that she wrapped in thin plastic overshoes.

He held out his hand as she reached him and she shook it firmly. Before he could mouth the friendly greeting that he had prepared, she got straight down to it. 'Is this how you found him?' Jones shot a startled glance at the inspector, who raised his hand to keep him quiet.

'More or less,' he lied. 'It could have been moved prior to our arrival, by them who found it, but it's roughly right.'

Doctor Sheila Peterson gave him a long dubious stare. 'Really!' She turned her gaze on Sergeant Jones, who shrugged helplessly. 'Well let's see what we've got,' she snapped. From her neat black leather bag she produced a pair of vinyl gloves and knelt down next to the corpse. As she did so her tight skirt rose up her legs slightly and the young sergeant made an almost audible gasp.

She pressed a switch on her Dictaphone with

a long, slender finger - adorned with a nail painted immaculately with deep red varnish. 'The body is of a man, in his mid to late thirties. Brown hair, slightly curling, not thinning yet. No distinguishing marks on the face. Eyes still open. Hands fairly clean, fingers and fingernails don't indicate that he was a manual worker, but faint traces of some sort of adhesive on the fingertips. The body is fully clothed, so no evidence of marks or damage to the skin. I'll be able to tell more when I get it back to the lab. Time of death, around two hours ago – around 9 am. A wound to the chest is the apparent cause of death. He would have been facing his assailant and so must have been able to see him. There are traces of vegetation on the front of the clothing that strongly suggest that he was face down when he fell!'

She looked up accusingly at the inspector who dismissed the comment with a wave of his hand. He barked at his junior, eager to change the subject and give the appearance of urgent competence. 'Get on the blower to HQ, son, and get a body bag brought down.' Then back to the pathologist, 'Thanks doc. We'll get it sent over to you.' He turned away, wishing her gone. But before leaving, she spoke to the sergeant.

'Accompany me back to the car, would you?' He nodded nervously. He wanted very much to make a good impression on her, but he suspected, correctly, that she wanted to ask some awkward questions. Before they could leave, an elderly gentleman, his walking stick waving in the air, his bald head bobbing excitedly, distracted them by breaking through the blue and white tape and walking up to the body. He was dragging a large and very fierce looking dog behind him.

'Officer!' he called out to the inspector. 'Trevor Thomson! Retired! Ex East Midland force! Living in the village! Just want you to know I'm around! Any help you need, just ask! Keen to get back in harness, don't you know! Can help with the interviews! They all know me! I'll help…'

The inspector made several attempts to stop this torrent of unwanted assertions of Trevor's possible usefulness, but Trevor was hard of hearing. Vanity meant that he never admitted this, never mind got a hearing aid. Several minutes of excited gabble passed before the inspector decided that drastic action was required. He stormed up to the unfortunate elderly gentleman, grabbed him by the collar of his shirt and yelled, projecting spittle into his face. 'GET YOUR BLOODY ARSE OUT OF THIS BLEEDING CRIME SCENE AND BUGGER OFF!' There was a shocked silence and then Trevor moved his face slightly closer to the inspector's and whispered, 'What?'

The senior officer raised a fist and Trevor scuttled away, back home, to tell his wife that he had offered his services and he was sure it had been well received. He would certainly be contacted soon.

The pathologist sat in her car with the door open and her long legs stretched out onto the field so that she could pull off the trainers and put on her normal shoes. The sergeant breathed in hard as he admired her shapely calves. 'What happened, Ken? He moved it, didn't he?'

The sergeant opted for a full confession. 'He made me do it. He thought the man had just dropped dead where he was.'

'He hoped. Less work for him. It's hardly likely, is it? He can't be much over thirty. How many thirty-year-olds drop dead in woods?'

'I know, but orders are orders.'

'I know. You're stuck with him. Best not to rock the boat. Your chance will come.'

'Any chance we could meet up? It's been a while…'

'It's complicated, as you know, Ken. Leave it for a while. I am working on it.'

'I miss you, Sheila.'

'Me too. Got to go. I'll have a report ready for you by tonight.'

'Bye then.' He made his way back to the crime scene deep in thought. The inspector was waiting impatiently.

'Wake up son! Beats me why she needs an escort back to her car, anyway!'

The sergeant thought quickly. 'She was worried that the killer might still be around, sir.'

The inspector span round, looking in all directions, slightly anxious. The tall trees, the leaf buds just beginning to turn green, waved to him as the breeze caught their branches. The sea of bluebells stirred, a beautiful haze of azure. He shrugged, 'You heard what she said. Time of death at least two hours ago. He'll be long gone by now.' They listened. There was no bird song.

Tiny insects scurried beneath the ground cover, but there was nothing to give away their presence. 'We'll leave a couple of men here to keep nosey parkers away from the crime scene. Let's get back to the office and get the investigation started!'

As they walked back to the car, the sergeant felt far from happy. He had no choice but to follow. He knew they should have had the immediate area searched thoroughly before any possible traces of the attacker or DNA samples were eroded by animal activity or weather.

The inspector opened the boot of his car and sighed as he saw the golf clubs lying there, forlornly. It could be a long time before they swung again in anger unless he could clear this business up swiftly. Less than a year left before retirement with a generous pension. Time had been passing painfully slowly recently.

Shortly after they had driven away from the crime scene, a black SUV drove slowly down the narrow lane leading to the woods, as if carefully feeling its way. It had two occupants. Both were male, with swarthy complexions, dressed in neutral, dark grey track suits. The car was steered slowly through the field gate and came to a stop a hundred years from the edge of the woodland. The two men stared at the police cars and lines of blue and white tape in the distance. Then, more quickly, turned back the way they had come. Tyres spinning, dust and grit flying up from the wheels as they made their escape.

As the SUV speeded towards the A31, the gentleman who had been unceremoniously ejected from the crime scene was making himself a centre of attention. Trevor was at the centre of a large group of neighbours stunned by the horror of what had happened in their idyllic, sleepy Dorset village. They listened agog as he told them how he had been allowed to approach the body and had offered his services to the officer in charge.

'I expect they'll be in touch any time now,' he asserted to his incredulous neighbours. 'Because of the police cuts. An extra pair of hands will be invaluable. Especially one as experienced as mine!'

If anyone needed to boost his reputation as a sleuth, it was Trevor. This was one of the reasons why his audience listened with a strong element of doubt. Any confidence his neighbours had in his abilities had shrunk to nothing during the coronavirus lockdown the year before. He had set himself up as a local vigilante, dedicated to keeping the village safe from interlopers who could bring the virus with them from distant parts and crack down on petty crime (of which there was none). During the course of his patrols, he had spied on a woman. He suspected her of being an interloper, breaking the lockdown rules. He tried to see who it was by peering through her caravan windows. She was actually a covid nurse who had been transferred to Dorchester hospital and so was staying in a friend's caravan. This almost got him arrested as a peeping tom.

Dennis, his closest neighbour, pressed Trevor for more details. 'Did you see the face? Did you recognise him? Was it someone local?'

For Trevor, this was no time for factual accuracy. He had an audience, hanging onto his every word. For a moment he was back in the force. He was reliving his other moment of drama and fame when he gave a press conference to a roomful of journalists. He was leading a crucial investigation into the Midlands Creeper, a serial thief who had been stealing women's underwear from washing lines all over

Dudley. His imagination in high gear, he drew himself up, took a deep breath and made an announcement that sent a chill of fear through his listeners' hearts. 'I couldn't be sure. There was a lot of blood. But I'm sure I recognised him. I'm sure he's someone who lives in the village. He must have been killed by someone we know. There's a murderer amongst us. No doubt about that!'

There was a collective gasp of horror. Annette gripped her husband's hand tightly. Martha clasped her hands in prayer. She was putting her faith in Someone much more reliable than Trevor. The good Lord was watching over her. He would ensure that if people were doomed to a violent death, His most loyal servants would certainly be saved.

Trevor realised that they were anxious. He was better at reading facial expressions than picking up words. He sought to reassure his neighbours. 'You're in safe hands. The Dorset force is already on top of this. And they've a one hundred per cent record in these cases. There haven't been any unsolved murders in Dorset for as long as I can remember!'

And this was true. To be absolutely accurate,

this was because there hadn't been any murders in Dorset for as long as he could remember. But there was even more reassuring news to give. 'And it won't just be the official force at work. They'll be getting my full support. So they'll have someone here on the ground with an intimate knowledge of the area!'

Oddly, the looks on the faces of his audience suggested that they were now less confident than they had been before. In fact, Freda Simpkins clutched his arm in alarm. 'What should we do? To be safe? Some of us…' and she looked round for confirmation, 'are women on our own.' Trevor's hearing wasn't good. He didn't catch what she said. Under normal circumstances, he would have uttered a brief 'what?' But amongst a group of what he mistakenly considered friends, he felt safe to be more informal.

'Eh?'

'We won't be safe in our beds! Do you think it would be best,' she said thoughtfully, 'if we moved in with other people? Those of us who are on our own? If we bunked up together? It might be safer…?' As Mrs. Simpkins weighed up the possibilities, her eye fell eventually on

Charles – a single man who, she thought, would certainly be safer if he 'bunked up' with her. Safer from the killer, anyway.

Although Charles lived a pedantic life, seeking grammatical error wherever he could detect it, especially in the writings of the rich and famous, and was generally immune from gossip, he had heard something of Widow Simpkins' reputation. As she gazed suggestively at him, Charles was already turning away and making his escape.

3

The two girls sat in tears on the edge of a bed. Doina was shaking, in a state of shock, and her friend, who clutched her hand tightly for comfort, was terrified. Over the course of twelve hours, they had been raped multiple times. It was vital to their keepers that they were broken in – adequately prepared for their life there.

A woman stood between them and the door. She was the trusty. In exchange for special treatment – fewer clients, more pocket money and no beatings – she kept the other girls in line. She was about to initiate them into their duties. But first, she had to make their situation absolutely clear. 'Listen up. You came here on forged papers. It cost the smugglers two thousand dollars each to bring you sluts here. You've that to pay back with interest before you can frigging leave. Get it? And don't even think of running or the frigging police. If they catch you, you're bloody done for. This country takes a frigging hard line on illegal immigrants. Prison, then you'll be deported. Back to your families in Romania. Sent back as criminal whores.' Doina broke down and burst into loud sobbing. The woman's tone softened. 'But be good girls and do what you're told and I'll look after you. Okay?'

Meanwhile, at Police Headquarters, Detective Inspector Longbottom sensed that a breakthrough in the case was imminent. A clue had emerged to the dead man's identity that might bring things to a swift conclusion.

Initially, it had been impossible to put a name to the corpse. A swift search of the body's clothing revealed no wallet, no driving licence, no credit cards. It had seemed to Dorset police's most experienced crime officer that the man had deliberately tried to keep his identity secret. This in itself was suspicious. The detective's nose for nefarious activity twitched, as it always did when he detected a deliberate attempt to conceal information. This man had been up to no good, he was certain of that.

He turned again to the plastic wrapped parcel that contained the dead man's clothing. It was then, from the back pocket of the trousers, came the discovery he needed. A small piece of card. He showed it in triumph to his assistant, Ken Jones. 'Here we go, son! Look at this!'

The sergeant did as he was bid. The object he was being asked to admire was a creased rectangle of card, about four centimetres by three, upon which was written: 'Tamiya Members Club, membership number 8452001.' He passed it back to his senior, with nothing more than a nod. He recognised that this could indeed be useful. It would mean that they could check with the club's membership records, find the man's name and probably his address. But the senior detective saw much more in it than that. It was the advantage gained from many years of experience in the pursuit of justice across the rolling fields of Dorset, seeking out sheep thieves and mislaid tractors.

The inspector's pinched, cynical face had creased into a triumphant grin. 'Tamiya Members Club, Jones! Tamiya! Chinese! A men's club! This'll be what's behind all this! Vice! A drugs ring! Lap dancers! So called escorts! We're onto something here son!'

As the inspector's hunches go, this one was

not so far off the mark. Only about three hundred miles, in fact, as the sergeant discovered when he googled 'Tamiya'. It wasn't Chinese. But it was close. It was Japanese. But as for the drugs and vice rings, well, a bit wide of the mark. To his superior's astonishment, it seemed that it was a firm that made plastic kits to make model aircraft. The sergeant had to scroll through page after page of plastic fighter jets, tanks, ships, and rockets before the detective inspector reluctantly agreed that this probably wasn't a cover for illegal activities.

'Shall I get in touch with the club, sir, to find who the man is?'

'Worth a try. Give it a go, lad.'

And it was at this point that the case began to unravel. Jones accessed the club's membership records and quickly established that their corpse had a name, Alec Bartle. And an address. In Bishop Farthing.

The inspector's fingers picked up a ball point pen, and, dreaming for just a moment that it was his favourite putter, he began to chew the end, deep in thought. It was at times like this that an experienced detective makes his mark, and he was about to pass on to his younger colleague some of the benefits of his many years of experience. 'This could be local, son. And where someone's killed or missing close to home, ninety-nine times out of a hundred, there's a family member involved. Check the parish records! Was he married?'

The sergeant was far from sure that parish records had been kept up to date for the last hundred years and so chose instead to scan the electoral roll. And there he was. Bartle Alec, Middle Cottage, Mapwood Row, Bishop Farthing, Dorset. And there was another name. Elyse. The inspector's piercing, watery eyes lit up. 'See if we've got anything on her, son! This could be it!'

And it, it certainly was. To the inspector's delight, Elyse Bartle was indeed on their criminal data base. In fact, she had been arrested only eighteen months before. And when the reason for the arrest shone out from the computer screen, the inspector fairly cooed with delight.

'Assault! Grievous bodily harm! And look – look who she attacked! Her husband, Alec Bartle! We've got her, son! We've got her bang to rights!'

Longbottom settled back in his seat, a smug smile on his face. It was the expression of a man for whom the world has fallen into place. He'd have this case sewn up by teatime. And here was a chance to impress his junior. He was about to make a prediction. Once he had been proved right, he would enjoy bathing in the awe and wonder that the sergeant would show as he admired his superior's cleverness.

'I'll tell you son. I'll tell you what we'll find. This woman failed to kill him at this first attempt. She's been let out by our rubbish prison system. She's followed the poor sod to the woods - or persuaded him to go for a walk there with her. She's smuggled a sharp knife from the kitchen and when he isn't watching, stabbed him with it! Straight through the chest! Typical domestic. Mark my words, son. Once we accost her, she'll be so riddled with guilt, she'll make a full and complete confession before a lawyer has a chance to interfere! Lawyers! Waste of bloody skin, every bloody one of them!'

Before his sergeant could read on to discover that the case had never come to court, that the case had been dropped and the couple reconciled, the inspector was grabbing his keys.

'We've got the address, lad! Let's get over there. No need for back-up, the two of us will be enough to bring her in! Got the cuffs?' Ken grabbed them from a drawer and hastily followed his exultant superior to their unmarked car.

D.I. Longbottom pressed his foot down on the accelerator and heard the powerful engine of the Jaguar roar into life. He loved moments like this – moments of power. It gave him a rush almost as high as the feeling he got when he holed in one at the par three on his local course. As the car purred into motion and he switched on the blue flashing lights, he felt the stimulation in his groin as the adrenalin raced through his body. As the years had taken their toll, this was now the only time he ever felt much stimulation in the groin area, but that problem was far from his thoughts as they raced down Dorset's narrow winding lanes towards their goal. Ken braced himself in his seat and silently prayed as they swung round blind bends, between tall hedges, with no idea what was around the corner and no room to manoeuvre out of the way if they met an oncoming tractor. The inspector turned on the siren as they neared Bishop Farthing village. He wanted to arrive in style.

The effect he wanted to create fell apart as they approached the edge of the collection of hamlets that make up the village. Was the house near here? They had a street address, but there did not seem to be any street signs. Most of the houses had names but finding the correct one in this warren of narrow lanes was going to be a slow and difficult business. After cruising round for several minutes and feeling rather stupid, they spied a lady walking a dog. D.I. Longbottom wound down his window. The woman's Labrador immediately jumped up, put his paws on the edge of the glass and peed on the door. This wasn't the impressive entry to Bishop Farthing that the officer had hoped for.

'Excuse me, ma'am – can you direct us to…' He turned to his sergeant who helpfully passed him a slip of paper. The D.I. fumbled in his pocket, found his reading glasses, and read out the address. The lady looked thoughtful. 'Sorry. I don't know all the house names. I'm fairly new, only lived here twenty years. Whose house is it?'

Detective Inspector Longbottom was cautious. He wasn't sure how much information he should reveal at this early stage in the investigation. Ken, however, assuming that the

D.I. had forgotten the name, chimed in. 'Her name's Elyse. Do you know her?'

'Oh yes, everyone does! Turn left at the war memorial and she's about fifty yards on the right! She won't be in, though. She'll be at work.'

'We'll call anyway, just in case,' said Longbottom, cautiously. 'And we'd appreciate it if you'd keep our interest to yourself, ma'am. It wouldn't be right to broadcast any of this at the moment. Confidential, right?' And having given this serious warning, he switched his blue lights back on. More confident now in the direction he was taking, he hoped still to make an impressive arrival. The lady lifted her phone from her bag and began telling everyone she knew that the police were here. Probably to do with the body in the wood. And they were heading for the home of Elyse Bartle. She wondered why. And so did everyone else!

The police car pulled up outside Middle Cottage and as it did so a crowd was already assembling. D.I.Longbottom instructed his sidekick to hold them back. 'Where've they bloody come from? Keep 'em back lad. I'll see if she's in!' He walked confidently up to the front door and knocked loudly. The sound echoed back to him from the dim interior. He knocked again, even more loudly, as if the firm demands for entry from an officer of the law should by rights be answered even by an empty house. Frustrated, he walked round to the back. Still no answer. He peered in through the kitchen window, perching himself inelegantly on a plant pot and causing considerable destruction to a large pelargonium planted within it. He wiped the condensation from the glass and peeped in, hoping to see pools of blood, a scene of chaos caused by a fight to the death or at least a few broken plates. Disappointingly, the kitchen was neat, clean, and even the breakfast pots washed on the drainer. He was not discouraged. It could be that the murder scene had been cleaned of prints.

Sergeant Jones joined him. 'They're keeping away, sir. They say she'll be at work. They're not sure where. It's one of the estate agencies in town.'

'OK, son. I'll drive into town and check them out. You stay here. In case she comes back. And I'll send a couple of men over to help you out. Do a door to door. See what you can found out!'

'Sir!'

Whilst these two pearls of the Dorset constabulary worked out their plan of action, they were being outclassed by the collective minds of the folk of Bishop Farthing. The neighbourhood website was humming like a hive of bees. Mrs. Fortnum at Fivepenny Hollow was sure she had heard gunshots in the night. Old Winston Giles at Four Acre Farm was woken by someone screaming at three a.m., but it might have been a cat. Several good folk on Orchard Row had it on reliable authority that more bodies had been found and the police were suspecting a Mafia-type mob killing. Geraldine on Pinchparson's Lane had followed a trail of blood out of her kitchen door and down the garden path. At the end of it, she found her neighbour's dog dining on her beef joint. Lower down the hill, at Pinchparson's Bottom two neighbours were debating whether or not to take down the village sign, to confuse the killer if he tried to strike again.

The inspector, unaware of the drama around him, had tracked down the agency where his chief, and only, suspect Elyse Bartle worked. He showed the value of his years of experience when he surrounded the premises with all the force he could muster before going in to challenge her. Police Constable Fred Binns, two months off retirement and with a gammy leg, was stationed at the rear of the premises in case she made a run for it. Woman Police Constable Gladys Pimm was to accompany him into the premises in case the suspect needed restraining. It could cause problems with the Police Complaints Commission if Inspector Longbottom found himself grappling with a female suspect. Gladys could do the job. She was the local force weightlifting champion. Men and women.

In the end, the arrest went smoothly. Elyse was at work in the office, fielding enquiries from city bound customers eager to escape to the country. One outcome of the pandemic, a realisation that you are probably safer away from high concentrations of people, meant that enquiries were still flocking in. D.I.Longbottom walked confidently up to her desk and checked he'd approached the right person. 'Elyse Bartle?' In truth, the name plate on the front of her desk was a bit of a giveaway, but it's better to be certain. Arresting someone by mistake and charging them with murder, then finding out that you have imprisoned the subject's best friend, can take a lot of living down.

'Elyse Bartle?'

'Yes, sir. Have you come about the one-bedroom flat in Wimborne? You're a few minutes early, but it's fine. We can leave now, if you like?'

'Afraid not, miss. I have to ask you to come along with me. You don't have to say anything, but anything you do say…'

Elyse went white. 'Oh my God! I knew this would happen! I've been feeling so guilty! Just let me grab my bag! Oh my God, I'm so sorry! I see now how wrong I was!'

Detective Inspector Longbottom smiled the smile of a man who has been very clever indeed and solved a case in a world record time. He would be famous throughout the force. He could retire on this. In fact, he intended to. He led the weeping Elyse to the car and pushed her head down in true policemanly fashion to steer her through the passenger door. The blue light went on. He radioed the rest of his team to tell them that the arrest had been successfully concluded. The lady policewoman was eyeing the photocopy machine wondering how high she could lift it, just for practice. Police Constable Fred Binns struggled to where his car was parked only to discover he'd been given a ticket for staying forty five minutes in a thirty-minute zone. He limped off to find the guilty traffic warden.

As Elyse wept her way to the police station, huddled in the back of the police car, some of her neighbours were assembling in the village hall. Trevor had summoned the folk of Bishop Farthing to a crisis meeting. The response had been mixed. Many were of the opinion that these matters were best left to the professionals. The rest were prepared to hear their own ex-professional out. Most hadn't turned up at all. And so it was seven brave folk who assembled at the hall and one of those was Trevor. He greeted each warmly and declared that they had best wait a few more minutes to see if any late comers were on their way. They weren't and so ten minutes late he began.

His proposal was simple and eminently sensible. There had been an unexplained death in the village. He was proud of his definition. Most were talking of a murder, but he was technically correct. No-one knew yet, he assured his audience, how the deceased had met his end, or who he was, and until the circumstances were determined by skilful detective work and an autopsy, this was simply unexplained. His audience, nodded, duly impressed by his expertise.

But for the moment, it would be safest to assume that a crime had been committed. They had a duty to ensure that their fellow villagers were safe. He had drawn up a rota. He would lead the six men and one woman assembled there as a defence force. They would patrol the streets of Bishop Farthing and watch out for any sign of suspicious activity. If they spotted the killer, they would send out an alarm to their neighbours so that they could lock down and wait for the Dorset police force to arrive. He looked round in triumph. This was his final moment of fame and glory. Why, he alone might capture the offender and make his name – with their help of course.

The village hall was large. It could hold a hundred people comfortably. The walls were painted a neutral shade of beige that started light and darkened as it moved up the walls, beyond the range of the cleaner. The metal struts that support the roof protect many small spiders that keep the building fairly clear of flies, except in the warmest summers. A bracket has been fastened to one of these metal beams to hold a projector, allowing the villagers to watch free film shows from a DVD machine. The spiders nest close to it so that they can enjoy the show. Spiderman movies are their favourites.

In this large space, the magnificent seven felt very insignificant. Trevor decided he had better bring the meeting to a swift conclusion. He had left the dog at home and it might be attacking his wife. 'So folks, who's interested? Whose names shall I put on the rota?' Then he remembered that he was truly hard of hearing. It was no wonder that he didn't hear their responses. He came up with a better plan. 'Put up your hand if you're ready to join! First patrol will be tonight!' There was an uneasy silence.

Dennis coughed and half raised his hand to speak. He then realised that this could be mistaken as a sign that he was volunteering and so withdrew it hurriedly. 'Are you sure this is a good idea Trevor? Could we perhaps contact the local police and ask them to organise a night patrol? I'm sure they'd be ready to help. Under the circumstances…'

There was an audible gasp of relief in the room. Suddenly, his five neighbours were of the same mind.

'They've got someone down in the wood anyway, guarding the site,' proffered Charles.

Freda Simpkins, who had at first been quite taken with the idea of wandering around in the night with male company, found that her courage failed her. 'Couldn't you phone them, Trevor? They'd listen to you!'

Trevor stared in despair as his posse dwindled down to nothing. He made one last attempt to shame them into co-operating. 'Well, I shall be out there.' His audience slinked guiltily away.

4

The villagers would have been heartened to know that, while they were failing to organise a defence force, the chief and only suspect was already in custody. D.I. Longbottom marched her into the police station in triumph. He beamed at the desk sergeant. 'Put this woman in a secure interview room, Sledge, until we're ready for her!' He turned to Elyse, smiling happily. After all, she had already confessed to the crime. Taking of statements would just be a formality. 'You'll need a solicitor, Mrs. Bartle. Have you got one, or shall we call the duty solicitor?'

'No!' she sobbed. 'I'll use the one I had last time!'

Longbottom guided her through the doorway to the interior of the station. He smiled again. She may have got you off last time, he thought, but I've got you bang to rights! You're going down for a long stretch this time!

With Elyse settled in a chair clutching a plastic water cup, he strolled to his office. It was time to acquaint the Chief Constable with his success and organise a press conference. News of an arrest had already leaked out somehow and reporters were gathering in the car park. Most had come directly from the crime scene. They weren't all happy. It had taken some time to find Bishop Farthing. It is too small and scattered to locate on a map. When they arrived, there had been little to see except trees and bluebells, scarred by the addition of a string of police tape. One television reporter had dropped a few things from her handbag at random in the undergrowth and the camera had panned over them slowly, as if they were clues of great significance. Others had heard of the meeting in the village hall and arrived just after it was aborted. Interviews had been useless. No-one seemed to know who the dead person was. The frustrated journalists were eager to get some real news.

As D.I. Longbottom emerged from the door of the police station and stood high on the steps to address them cameras rolled, and microphones were thrust into his face. He beamed out at the assembly. No new movie star taking his first steps on the red carpet at an Oscar ceremony could feel quite as proud and important as he did at that moment.

Questions flew around him like a murmuring of starlings. 'Have you identified the body?' 'Have you made an arrest?' 'Was this a sex attack?' (They hoped so. The more sensational the better.) 'Was the body naked?'

D.I. Longbottom raised a hand and the organs of the media fell silent. It is hard to imagine the sense of power he felt as stopped the tide of questions with an ease that would have amazed Canute. 'I have a short statement to make and then I will answer questions. First, two walkers came across a body in the bluebell woods at the village of Bishop Farthing. We arrived at the scene at ten a.m. this morning and ascertained that foul play had been involved. At twelve fifteen we brought in a thirty-three-year-old female for questioning, and she is helping us with our enquiries. We are not looking for anyone else in connection with this incident and we want to send our assurances to the local people that they are in no danger!'

He finished with a flourish and made a show of answering questions, pretending that there was much more he knew, but was prevented by legal restrictions from sharing. He congratulated himself on his success and went back indoors for coffee and a plate of biscuits. Soon he was on the phone contacting his golf buddies. He saw no reason why he shouldn't be back on the course the next afternoon. Meanwhile, there had been no success contacting Elyse's lawyer. She was in court that afternoon and wouldn't be available until the following morning. His chief suspect was popped into a cell for the night.

There was also a delay in the carrying out of the autopsy. Doctor Sheila Peterson had a pre-arranged meeting that meant she was out of the mortuary until later that evening. Rather surprisingly, the meeting was taking place in her bedroom. It was with the Chief Pathologist, her boss.

She had come to wonder how it was that she was given her current post. She hoped that it was because she was well qualified and interviewed well. A month into the job she began to suspect that the fact she was single, young and attractive might have influenced the decision in some small way. At first Harold had been attentive and helpful. Sheila had been grateful. After a particularly long day, he had invited her out for a drink after work. It would have been rude to refuse.

He was unlike all the (much younger) men that she had been out with before. Harold was mature, interesting, had a droll sense of humour and – most important of all – was more interested in talking about her than himself. He encouraged her to chat about her hopes, her ambitions, her family and political views. He was a good listener, offering intelligent and sensible comments and advice at appropriate intervals. The time had passed quickly. She had found it relaxing and easy to open up to him. Three glasses of wine later he had called a taxi for her, paid in advance, and wished her goodnight. It had all been friendly and gallant. She was impressed.

When he repeated the invitation the following week, she was happy to accept.

He took her to the same bar – she began to regard it as their special place – and the conversation was, again, comforting and relaxing. But this time it had been more about him. He had explained that he had married twice. The first had been to his childhood sweetheart from school. The first few years had been happy and they had been blessed with two fine children, both boys, who had taken much of his love and care. After ten tears of marriage, he discovered that she had been unfaithful. He was often away, acting as consultant pathologist in areas where the police were understaffed. One fateful week, he returned a day earlier than he had intended. His wife was not at home, but there was evidence in their bedroom of another man having shared it with her.

When she returned to their home later that afternoon, she was in a stranger's car. They came in laughing together, not realising that her husband was home. A dreadful scene followed. At the end, he told her that she should choose, between him and this new man in her life.

Sheila never suspected that he was practised at telling this story. She noted the tremble in his voice and felt a warm surge of compassion. He choked as he told her that his wife's decision to reject him for another had shattered his self-confidence. Sheila placed her hand over his at this point, squeezing it gently and sympathetically.

For several years he had lived alone, seeing his sons once a week and watching them moving gradually more and more distant from him. Harold confessed that he had tried brief flirtations with new partners, but whenever they became serious, he would panic, believing that these relationships too would go wrong, and his heart would be broken again.

Sheila saw his eyes fill as he recalled these difficult times and was close to tears herself. Then, he told her, he had met Margot. She was so unlike his first wife. At first, she was a sympathetic ear and a comfort. She began to care for him. His work was taking up much of his time. He needed someone to attend to cleaning, washing clothes and shopping. It wasn't a romantic arrangement. She just volunteered to help. He came to depend on her more and more. They began to embrace, it was almost maternal, and eventually she moved in with him.

'I felt I could trust her. I'm not sure I could tell you why…'

'Just something about her?'

'Well, to be honest, she's…homely.'

'Homely?'

'Sounds bad, doesn't it?'

'Oh, you mean…'

'She's not really femme fatale material. She was what I needed at the time. Someone reliable. I was travelling a lot. She was always there, looking after the house…and me.'

'But not, how shall I put it? Everything you needed.'

'You're a very perceptive girl!' He poured them both another glass of Sauvignon Blanc. 'No. Not everything I need. You can probably tell what's missing.'

'I can guess.'

'We're already discussing separation. Obviously, it will lead on…to divorce. But it's not to be rushed. It's fairer to take in it in easy steps.'

'Easy? For both of you?'

'Not entirely. I think she feels I'm her only chance. She's not the most attractive of women. That's a terrible thing to say, I know. But it's true. She'll cling on as long as she can. But a loveless marriage is best ended, even though it hurts.'

'I can tell it's not easy for both of you.'

He gazed into her eyes and put both his hands over hers as if he was sheltering a delicate butterfly. And when they parted that evening, their goodbye kisses were no longer pecks on the cheek.

So here Sheila was, in a relationship with her married boss that on his side was becoming more and more important to his happiness, but, on her side, was beginning to pall. He wasn't exactly old enough to be her father. He claimed only fifteen years on her (though she had her doubts). He was thinning a little and greying a lot. She was beginning to feel embarrassed when they were seen out together, as if she were out with her dad. The music he liked was popular before she was born, and he had no sympathy with hers.

There were other matters that concerned her even more. Harold told her he'd undergone a vasectomy after his two sons were born. She had said nothing, but this upset her. Sheila was young enough to want children of her own.

He promised her that the operation could be reversed. Unknown to him, she checked this on the internet. What she discovered was not good. Vasectomy reversal is rarely allowed on the NHS. If they agree, there could be a very long wait. Vasectomies could be done privately but this costs thousands of pounds. Harold was not a wealthy man. Could he afford it? And if he did, it's highly unlikely to be effective. Harold had been snipped twenty years ago. Scar tissue would have built up and blocked the route for sperm. The more she thought about it, the more hopeless it seemed.

And so, Sheila was seriously considering ending her relationship and her determination had grown stronger since she met Ken Jones. He was close to her age, good looking, sensitive and intelligent (rare qualities in a man, she had found), and unsnipped.

But convincing Harry they should call it a day was proving incredibly difficult. The more she hinted that she wanted a break, the more he asserted that she was the one for him and he was ready to leave his wife whenever Sheila gave the word. Their meetings had once been exciting, but now, as she showered and prepared to go back to work, she felt depressed and deflated.

5

Detective Sergeant Ken Jones was at that moment organising door to door enquiries in the village of Bishop Farthing, with no idea of the range of eccentricities that these good people would present. He chose to begin at the home of Trevor, whose offer to help in the investigation had been so rudely rejected by his senior colleague. As he was greeted warmly at the door by the ex-policemen, D.C. Jenny Grace was encountering Muriel. This lady lived opposite Trevor and had no reason to be complimentary about him.

Muriel invited the detective constable in and gestured to a chair. Of medium height, in dark navy slacks and a rich maroon top, Jenny never thought herself attractive, but she was selling herself short. Her hair was stunning, black, thick and curly. Her eyes were dark, her lips full, her skin the colour of hot chocolate. The lady constable accepted the offer of a seat with a polite smile.

Muriel sat opposite and crossed her arms in a challenging manner. She was a well-built woman with severely cut, greying hair, an old tweed skirt that had begun to stretch across the spread of her buttocks and a brown and green cardigan that was fraying around the edges. Her fingernails were black and her fingers brown from labour in the garden. If her interviewer had looked out at the garden behind the house, she would have seen no flowers. Muriel had no interest in such fripperies. She was a rearer of vegetables – of substantial size. Muriel was the founder member of the Bishop Farthing Gardening Club.

Once a year they would hold a flower show. Muriel's vegetables were always a source of jealousy and awe. Behind her formidable presence, ranged along the mantlepiece, was a line of impressive trophies, all of which had been donated by the proud owner in the confident knowledge that every year they would be won by her. There was the cup for the best leeks, a trophy for the best cucumber, one for the best hamper of produce, a cup for the best display of salads. In centre place, catching the sunlight stealing in through the window and dazzling anyone who gazed at it, was the largest trophy of all. This was the cup for the best overall performance in the vegetable section of the show.

Members who grew flowers and who displayed them in the best flower arrangement; the finest three specimens of annuals; or the best perennial display would be awarded a certificate if they were successful. As founder and chair of the club, Muriel was reluctant to share her glory. She had stubbornly resisted any move to purchase cups for mere flower displays.

She expected visitors to be impressed by her array of silver ware, but the Detective Constable made no comment. She got straight to the point.

'Could I start by getting your name for my records?'

A simple question, but Muriel was not going to waste her time with trivialities. 'I see he's gone in across the road!' Muriel was old fashioned enough to believe that Jenny's colleague, being male, would be her superior. On this single occasion she was correct. And she assumed that he was the one who was tracking down the suspects in the case,

'Yes. That's my colleague, Detective Sergeant Jones. He's gone there because we believe that the gentleman who lives there may be able to provide us with useful information.'

Muriel relaxed back in her chair, a broad smile on her face. Never had she had more faith in the detective qualities of our police force. 'Oh yes. He's gone to the right place, no doubt about that!'

The page on Jenny's pad was still blank. She had so far failed to get even the name of this lady. But her ears pricked up at this. 'Why do say that?'

Muriel raised one hand and tapped a finger, blackened from years of soil and compost (why are gardeners described as green fingered? I've never met a green fingered one yet) and tapped the digit knowingly against the side of her nose. 'They'll be behind this. Somehow. Crackers, the pair of them!'

'Pardon, ma'am?' surprised but ready, Jenny poised the tip of her ball point pen a centimetre from the page, just in case Muriel had vital information to tell.

The lady leaned forward – she clearly had something of importance to impart. Muriel almost whispered her response. 'Bent!'

Jenny scribbled excitedly. 'They're bent? What do you mean, madam? They're crooks?'

Muriel leaned back – a smile of satisfaction on her face to have an audience for her concerns at last. 'Yes bent. Their carrots. They couldn't grow a straight one if their lives bloody well depended on it!'

Meanwhile, Detective Sergeant Jones knocked on Trevor's door. From inside the house, he heard a dog barking loudly. Thumps and scrapes as the beast scratched and threw himself against the door. Minutes passed as someone indoors tried to control the dog and finally a harassed looking Trevor nervously opened the door a few inches.

'Afternoon.' The detective flashed his police ID. 'I wonder if you could spare a few minutes to talk about this morning?'

'Yes! Yes, of course! Cassie! It's the police inspector, love!' Trevor only called his wife Cassie on her birthday and at Christmas and not always then. There was the sound of furtive scurrying as she concealed plasticine dolls with long pins stuck in them. To her, they represented neighbours that she had issues with. To anyone else they looked like…lumps of plasticine. Trevor opened the door wider. He was delighted: certain that this visit was a direct result of his offer to help, him being an experienced professional.

'Come in! Come in! This is my wife, Cassandra! And this is…sorry, I didn't get your name!'

'Detective Sergeant Jones. Ken Jones.'

Trevor beamed and turned to address his wife. 'Ben Holmes, dear. He wants my advice on the investigation. You'd better go in the kitchen, love.'

'I'm sure she could stay.'

'That's right. Been in all day. Haven't you, dear?'

Cassandra shuffled away, exiling herself in the back of the house. Ken sighed and thought this was going to be very hard work indeed. Resignedly he pulled out his notebook and prepared to write. 'Now, mister..?'

'No…there's no sister. Just me and the wife.'

Ken tried again, a little louder. 'Your name? I need your name for my notes.'

'Oh yes! Of course! Why didn't you say? It's Thomson. Without a pee. There's no pee. Trevor Thomson. I was with the West Midlands Constabulary for thirty years. High up, you know.'

Ken nodded. 'Thank you. Very helpful.' He wasn't surprised that they'd taken the pee out of him. 'Now just for the record, can I ask where you were between eight and ten o'clock this morning?'

Trevor looked shifty. He drew Ken away from the kitchen door. He glanced towards it, a worried look on his face. 'Went out for a drive. In the car,' he whispered, conspiratorially. 'But I've got to be honest. If you cross check this with Cassandra, she'll tell you something different. Sounds suspicious I know.'

Ken began to respond, in a loud voice that was necessary to ensure that Trevor would understand. 'Why will she…' But Trevor silenced him with an agitated wave of his hand.

'Shhh! She doesn't know! You see, she thinks

I do odd jobs to help folks out… I'm a bit of a handyman you see. Dab hand with a screwdriver. Don't mind tackling a bit of wiring. And I do sometimes!' he asserted. 'Every now and again. Fix a shelf for an old dear down Sodom Lane. She's in a wheelchair now. It's all too much for her. But not every day. Sometimes I just drive off and park up. It gets me out of the house!' He winked at Ken. 'Gives me a bit of peace. Have a smoke. Read the Daily Mail. You know how it is. You married?'

Ken shook his head. 'Just for the record then, sir – did you hear or see anything suspicious at any time this morning? Anything unusual, that looking back on it may seem a little strange?'

Trevor Thomson, late of the West Midlands Constabulary, waved the detective to a chair. 'Well, now you're talking! Where to start?'

As Detective Sergeant Jones and D.C. Grace were gradually discovering the full scale of the problem they faced getting any sense out of the good people of Bishop Farthing, Detective Inspector Longbottom was receiving a surprise visit from on high. Literally. The police helicopter landed on the spare ground behind the station and no less a person than the Chief Constable walked from it, a beaming smile on his face.

Longbottom straightened to attention. 'Sir!'

'Relax, Longbottom! As you were! I understand you've made excellent progress on this Bishop Farthing business?'

'Sir! Suspect arrested and safely in custody, sir!'

'Well done, Cyril! The whole unpleasant business tied up in record time! This is the type of efficient detective work that makes the force look good in the press. And, of course, it puts the public's minds at rest. Good work! Good work! I'll put a commendation in your record for this!'

'Sir!'

The Chief half turned to go and then, as if as an afterthought, 'Oh by the way, Cyril. It hardly matters now. Not relevant of course. But I had a call from Old Grumble this morning. You know him, don't you? He was Grand Master of the lodge a couple of years ago. He'd heard about this unpleasantness in Bishop Farthing. His patch, you know. He just wanted to check that we wouldn't be involving the manor house in it. It's a difficult time for him. Staffing problems. Didn't want the place disturbed. And he's in his eighties, of course. Peer of the realm. I can get back to him, can I? Assure him none of your boys and girls will be sniffing round the ancestral pile?'

D.I. Longbottom shot to attention again. 'Indeed so, sir! My word, sir!'

'Good man! And I can expect a full report on my desk soon, can I?'

'By tomorrow morning, sir! The woman made a full confession as soon as I confronted her!'

'A woman, eh? My god, what's the world coming to? Ah well. Tomorrow morning then, Cyril?'

'Sir!'

And they parted, with a very secret handshake.

6

Dusk was falling as Sheila walked to the mortuary. She was much later than she had hoped. The parting from Harold after their afternoon together had been long drawn out and stressful. He was becoming more demanding at a time when she was feeling less and less inclined to be intimate with him. His need for her was concerning. Making a clean break would be easier if he were not her boss. And she felt that she owed him a lot. Would she have got this post – one she treasured – without his influence? And she owed even more to him than that. He had taught her much about her needs and sensuality, more than she'd even guessed at before.

Sheila was preoccupied with this predicament as she scrubbed and gowned in the empty, echoing mortuary before her professionalism took over and she walked briskly to the slab.

The corpse had been stripped and the items of clothing bagged ready for forensics. The body was stiff, covered totally by a white sheet. She peeled this down to the waist and began immediately to record her findings on her digital recorder. Estimate of age, sex, colour of hair, condition of skin – the details purred out of her like a well-oiled machine. Then she turned her attention to the wound in the chest. Puzzled, she reached for a scalpel.

Detective Sergeant Jones and Detective Constable Grace drove back to the station at the end of a gruelling day. They laughed together as they recounted the details of their door-to-door interviews. The plan had been to cover most of the inhabitants in one afternoon, but they had barely achieved three encounters each. Never had they encountered such talkative people. These folk had so much gossip to impart about their neighbours that it proved impossible to halt the flow. Jenny had the misfortune to move, from Muriel's, to the lady who lived next door. Martha. She met Jenny at the door to her home, clutching a Bible to her ample bosom.

'Good afternoon. My name is Detective Constable Jenny Grace. I wonder if I could come in and ask you a few questions about anything you might have seen this morning?'

Martha moved aside so that Jenny could squeeze past and pointed her towards one of the armchairs in her living room. Then she left her to make a pot of tea. Martha had very few visitors. To be brutally honest, Martha had not shared her front room with another human being for more than a year and she was determined to make the most of this one. She did not need mortal company of course. God was a constant presence in her home.

'Let me ask you something before we start.' Martha collected two teacups and saucers from the dresser and was selecting an attractive range of chocolate biscuits. It was an effort to move around. She had been in bed for weeks, cared for by Dennis's wife Annette, who called in two or three times a week and did a little shopping for her. She didn't need much. She was preparing for the second coming.

Constable Jenny Grace was touched by her kindness. She opened her notepad, pencil poised, and took a long look at Martha. Worryingly, Martha did not seem to have been to a hairdresser for a considerable time. And had not bought any items of clothing, if what she wore today was any guide, since 1959. Jenny began to wonder if this was a waste of time. She was tempted to call social services.

'Yes, of course. What would you like to know? Is it about our investigation?' Jenny asked, relaxing into the chair.

'No…no. I'm sure that's going well. Though I expect you've got a lot to do.' Her eyes glimmered as she stared at Jenny, darkly. 'There's so much sin round here, after all…'

'Pardon?'

'That's why you've come, isn't it? I'm not surprised, love. I knew there'd be a reckoning some day!' She sank into an adjacent armchair and poured the tea. 'But let me ask you this, love.'

Jenny was on guard. There was only so much that she was allowed to reveal about how the investigation was going. She sat upright, alert to danger, 'Yes, of course ma'am. What is it you want to know?'

Martha leaned toward her, picked up a large leather-bound book, and whispered, 'Have you given your soul to Jesus, my dear? Have you been saved?'

As they pulled into the station carpark, Jenny and Ken laughed again at their joint experiences. 'Did you get anything useful at all?' Ken asked, with a wry smile.

'Enough to fill a magistrates' court for weeks,' joked Jenny. 'There are children across the road who scare cats; a woman who hangs her underwear out to dry for everyone to see; a couple called Peter and Beth who are living in sin and she thinks the vicar is a homosexual. It seems we've walked into a hotbed of crime!'

It was getting late, so Ken dropped Jenny next to her car and then parked by the station entrance. He needed to check whether there was any message from Sheila. He expected some information on the case they were working on. He dreamed that she might send him an invitation to meet.

The duty sergeant was still on the desk. He was the only other person at the station as Ken checked the messages stored on his office phone. Yes, one was from Sheila. He ignored the others and went straight to it. 'Hi Ken. I've completed my initial findings. I'll be here until ten. Ring me when you're free!'

The chance to talk to Sheila, even if it was only on official business, was good. Ken dialled her number.

'Hi Sheila! How's it going? There's no rush, by the way. The D.I. thinks he's cracked the case. He's got the man's wife in custody!'

'He has? I didn't know. I've been …occupied all afternoon,' she said, discreetly.

'He thinks she'll have done it with a kitchen knife. Went down to the wood with him. Or sneaked up on him.'

'Really? What's her name? Annie Oakley?'

The joke was lost on Ken. 'No -uhmm – Elyse I think…'

'Well, she's a good shot. The man was brought down by shotgun from about eighty yards. The shell is embedded in his spine. That's why the injury was only visible from the front!'

'You're not joking, are you?'

'No. Definitely not.'

'We haven't interviewed the wife yet. She was waiting for her preferred solicitor. My god.

This could be an almighty cock up. I'd better talk to her now. If you're still there later, I'll come over.'

'Be good to see you. It's a bit lonely and morbid here. Bye!'

Ken out down the phone and let the implications of this sink through his consciousness like heavy mud sinking through a stagnant pool. Could Elyse really have shot her husband with a shotgun? How could she from such a distance unless she was an experienced shot? And if she hadn't, why had she confessed? He strode back to the desk and told the duty sergeant that he needed to see the prisoner, now.

As they opened the door of the cell, Ken felt disturbed and anxious. He had been worried from the start at the peremptory approach that the D.I. had taken. From their arrival on the crime scene, he had not followed the book. He had moved the body before the pathologist arrived and without adequate photographic evidence being secured. The immediate area had been screened off before they arrived, but they had not done a thorough search of the surroundings. If the fatal shot had come from a distance away as the pathologist claimed, all evidence might already have been lost.

Elyse was curled up on the hard bench that served as a bed and her face was streaked with tears. Her work suit was crumpled – the tight skirt drawn up slightly at the knees because of the foetal position she had curled into. Ken tried hard to convey the sympathy he genuinely felt.

'Mrs. Bartle – is there anything we can do to make you more comfortable?' She shook her head and began to weep, her body shaking with grief. He sat beside her, careful to ensure that no part of his body touched hers. He would have liked to put an arm around her, but to have done so could have been misinterpreted. 'I know that your chosen solicitor can't be with you until tomorrow morning, but there are questions I'd like to ask just to clear up any misunderstandings. Would you like me to call a duty solicitor?'

Elyse shook her head. It was difficult to make out her words through the sobs. 'No. I'm so sorry. I know it was wrong. If I could live it over again…'

Ken softened his voice, 'Elyse, can you tell me – have you a shotgun at home? Or access to one?'

Her eyes opened wide in surprise. 'No! Why?'

'It's just come up in our enquiries. You've absolutely no need to worry if you haven't got one. We may need to search your home, but if you're telling the truth, you don't need to be concerned!' He studied her carefully. If she was being totally truthful, and had nothing to hide, then her face would show it. Nothing registered – except confusion. Ken was the one worried now. He knew that his boss had messed up badly. And it could backfire on him if he didn't do as much as he could to rescue the situation. And the situation immediately became very much worse when Elyse, through her tears, made a very reasonable request. 'Could I call my husband?'

'I beg your pardon?'

'I know I've been lucky to have two happy years, but he must have decided to call it a day. I really hoped that he could forgive and forget, but I know I don't deserve it. I just want to tell him how truly sorry I am!'

'Sorry about?'

'Sorry for what I did to him that put him in hospital. I was mean and stupid. I was so lucky that he didn't press charges in the end. But if he's changed his mind – well – it's what I deserve, I suppose!'

'So when you told D.I.Longbottom that you were guilty, you were referring to…?'

'What I did in the lockdown. It just got on top of me. I must have been mad. But I was having an affair, you see. He was so not worth it! I see it now! But being in a lockdown with Alec when I wanted to be with someone else… And he was so controlling! I just lost it!'

'So you were admitting you were guilty to what you did two years ago?'

'Yes. Isn't that what you thought?'

The enormity of the mistake was now only too obvious to Ken. The cowardly way forward would be to withdraw and leave it to his boss to tell Elyse the terrible news. But he couldn't do that. For one thing, he didn't trust the D.I. to handle this at all well.

'Elyse, there's something I've got to tell you.'

'Yes?'

'When D.I.Longbottom took you into custody, he thought you'd hurt your husband again.'

'No! Never!'

'I'm afraid you must prepare yourself for some very distressing news.'

Clouds swept over Elyse as she cowered in the cold cell, waiting for Ken to tell her the news. Her first concern was for the trouble that Alec must be in to bring him to the attention of the police. It could be he'd fallen foul of the Inland Revenue. He was always cutting it fine when dealing with clients' tax affairs. The clouds of worry and doubt drifted past, each one darker than the one before. He might have committed a crime – and he was under arrest. Or he was ill. In hospital. As she stared into Ken's eyes the grey clouds were sent scurrying away across her sky and even darker and more threatening ones, full of the deep dark thunder of grief, took their place. An accident? A car crash? Was he seriously injured? On life support? Then total darkness fell upon her as Ken whispered, 'I'm so sorry. We found him this morning. Found his body.'

Elyse couldn't speak. Shock clutched at her throat and stifled her breath. Ken waited a few seconds. Then, 'You didn't know, did you?'

She shook her head, helplessly.

'I'm sorry, Elyse. I must ask you this. Where were you this morning? Between eight and nine o'clock?'

She stared back at him, with empty eyes. When she spoke, it was automatic. She had no need to give her reply any thought. 'On my way to work. At the office. I have to be in for eight thirty.'

Ken was experienced enough to know, without needing to check her alibi, that she was telling the truth. 'It's late, I know. But if there's anyone we can call – a friend? We'll get you a bereavement counsellor of course. Someone trained to help you.'

He got back to his desk. He couldn't release her. She'd been officially taken into custody, though not yet charged. Anyway, this late in the evening, where could she go? He would need to contact his boss, but he wasn't answering his phone. First thing in the morning he'd get a forensic team to do a thorough search of the crime scene. What a mess. They had a suspect who not only had not killed her husband - she did not even know he was dead. There could be serious repercussions. But before worrying about that he had to get the investigation back on course. He issued all the necessary orders and instructions and then drove to the mortuary. And Sheila.

7

Sheila was wrapping everything up as Ken arrived. The chilled air and the fluorescent tube lighting did not create a romantic environment, but he still felt a tremble of excitement as she pulled the surgical mask from her face and smiled in welcome. She had a plastic bag in her right hand and held it up for him to see.

'This is what remains of the shell. I'll send it to forensics and see if they can match it up. It was lodged in the spine, but I managed to get it out unharmed. If the shooter had been closer, it would have gone right through him.'

Ken nodded in acknowledgement.

'There was extensive plant material on the face from where the victim fell forward into the undergrowth. I'm afraid it proved that the body was interfered with before I arrived.' She shrugged her shoulders.

Ken smiled back, contritely. 'Well, if the wrong person has been arrested, turning the body will be the least of our worries.'

'None of it is your fault. If you need any back-up, I'll be here to support you. I saw Longbottom on the TV. He's going to look an idiot in the morning!'

There was still a trace of loyalty left in Ken. He was part of a team, after all. And there was no guarantee that he would not be dragged down with his boss. 'There's no way it could have been his wife who shot him?'

'The temperature of the body means that he was killed between eight and nine – probably closer to nine.'

'Then she would have been at work, or on her way to the office. She started at half eight in Yeovil.'

'Impossible then.' Sheila felt neither affection nor loyalty for D.I. Longbottom. He had been a thorn in her side for too long. He showed her no respect. She was sure it was because she was young and a woman. And she knew that he cut corners whenever he could. She would have no regrets if she brought the man down.

'It couldn't have been a lucky shot?'

Sheila laughed. It was the first time that day. 'The shot was fired by an expert. The shooter was at least eighty yards away. He was someone who shoots regularly – probably on organised pheasant shoots or at clay pigeons. The victim saw him and had started to turn away.' Sheila mimed the action. 'The bullet went through the left side of the chest, fracturing two ribs. Then it grazed the heart, ripping it open, before embedding itself in one of the vertebrae. It couldn't have been more accurate. He died instantly.'

Ken let this sink in. It had been a long day and he had a bad feeling that tomorrow would be even longer. Still, Sheila looked amazingly attractive, even in the regulation plastic body suit. 'Any chance of a drink? We could stop at The Antelope?'

She shook her head with, he thought, just a trace of regret. 'It's too soon. Ken. It's just too complicated. Give me time, eh? Leave me to sort things out. Then – maybe!'

'It was only the offer of a drink,' he joked,

'not an offer of marriage!'

She put one long, elegant finger on his lips. 'We both know where this is going. Just be patient. Please.'

'You can't blame me for trying.'

'I'd be disappointed if you didn't!'

Ken drove home feeling disconsolate. He understood how Sheila felt. She wanted a clean break from her previous lover before they could begin to think seriously about each other. He had no idea who his rival might be, only that he was, apparently, difficult to be rid of. He felt guilty about Jenny, Jenny Grace, the only woman constable on his team. She was a nice person, easy to get on with, and they had much in common because of their shared roles in the police force. They had flirted a little when she first joined them, a year ago. It was just light-hearted, nothing serious. He didn't think either of them actually meant any of it. It happened that they were the only two single people on the team and so it had seemed natural. They had exchanged messages on social media, but only idle chatter.

Then the team party last Christmas. They'd

met up at the Botany Bay on the Poole road. Wine had flowed and the atmosphere was relaxed and easy going. As the party broke up, he offered to share a taxi with Jenny. When they reached her apartment, she suggested that he got out as well and stay the night. They were both tipsy and they did sleep together.

It wouldn't have happened if they hadn't both been drunk. He thought they both understood that. He'd left the next morning and they had never spoken of it again. He should have talked to her. He should have said something. But time went on, month after month, always silent, not a word about what happened. It was like a secret between them, but one never referred to by either of them. The longer the silence lasted, the more certain he became that she felt the same as he did – that it was just a one-night stand, fuelled by alcohol. But every once a while – not often – hardly ever – he caught Jenny looking at him as if she was expecting him to say something, Anything, He didn't know what. And the moment would pass and they'd just be colleagues again. Just two detectives on the same team.

He pulled onto the drive of the two-bedroom starter home he was purchasing near Blandford Forum. There was no welcoming light. No-one to greet him. He turned the key in the lock and switched the main lights on. His hours of work made it impossible to keep a pet. He could have had a hamster, maybe, but he wasn't into rodents. Ken went straight to the television just to bring some life and sounds into his home. He phoned an order for a pizza and took a beer from the fridge. The late local news was on. He listened grimly as the reporter told of the discovery of a body in Bishop Farthing woods. The news item had been recorded when there was still daylight and the camera panned across the beautiful woodland, the heady blue haze of the bluebells and the fresh green of the new leaves just bursting from the branches. It scanned the police vehicles parked on the perimeter and the police tape strung between the trees. Ken shook his head as the reporter reassured the viewers that the police had the matter in hand. A suspect had been arrested and was helping them with their enquiries. The police were not apparently looking for anyone else regarding this enquiry and the public had nothing to fear.

Ken knew that no-one had actually been

arrested or charged and that in the morning there would have to be some embarrassing backtracking. He'd called the D.I. several times with no success to prepare him for tomorrow. Thursday night was his lodge meeting and so this was one time he was never available. He wouldn't be happy when he discovered that his case was far from closed and his prime suspect was almost certainly innocent. There was a knock on the door. His pizza had arrived. He opened another beer.

In a large run-down house only walking distance from where the container ships dock in Southampton, the two girls were being prepared for their first night working for their minders. They sat shivering in the reception room dressed in skimpy underwear. They knew they had to smile at the clients when they queued at the door. If they didn't get enough tricks, if Christina thought they were deliberately trying to evade attention, they would be taken upstairs and beaten savagely. Trembling, they did their best to look eager for sex.

Doina tried to distract her mind from what was happening. She imagined herself back in her homeland. She was standing at the door of their wooden house. Behind her, mama and her nan were preparing the meal. Her little brothers and sisters were playing in the wildflower meadows. Small fluffy clouds drifted slowly across the sky. Distant mountains were tipped with snow. How she wished she'd never left. They would have coped somehow. They lived frugally. She could have earned something.

A bulky man in a loose-fitting, soiled anorak, sporting an unkempt black beard, pointed at Helena. Doina wept for her friend but sighed with relief. Christina checked what service he wanted and took the cash. Helena led him up the stairs, sick in the stomach at what she was about to do.

8

That same evening, the people of Bishop Farthing listened with some sense of reassurance to the newscasts, but also with an increasing feeling of perplexity. No-one knew the identity of the unfortunate person dead in the woods. They couldn't work out who would have committed such a crime. The idea that it was one of their own was disconcerting to say the least. For once they were grateful for the sight of Trevor and his fierce dog patrolling the darkening lanes. Beth and Peter had stayed together all day, expecting that they would be visited by the police so that they could give their account of the discovery of the body. Surprisingly, no-one had called. As it reached ten p.m. Peter made to leave. It was not their night to stay together, and he had a lecture to prepare for the next morning. He kissed Beth goodnight, warned her to keep her doors firmly locked and felt reasonably safe for them both as he began the ten-minute walk back to his home. He passed Trevor on patrol.

'Night, Peter!'

'Goodnight! It all seems safe?'

'Nothing to worry about! The police've got the whole thing tied up! Suspect arrested! We've no need to worry!'

'Obviously not! Keep up the good work, then!'

'Will do!'

And Peter continued on his way, now in total darkness. There are no streetlights in Bishop Farthing. Occasionally a security light would come on as he passed the house of a cautious homeowner, but otherwise he had only his familiarity with the route to guide him. The black shapes of huge trees towered over him, blotting out even the stars. A cat scurried from a pitch-black hedge and made him start. As he reached his own gate and felt for the latch, he was vaguely uneasy. It had all been too quick. Too easy. He looked nervously round into the darkness. Was the killer truly in custody? Or did death still lurk in the quiet lanes of their idyllic village?

The light in the cell had been turned low for the night. Elyse lay on the hard bench that served as a bed, half asleep and half awake. She could hear the large clock over the counter in the police station ticking away the seconds of her incarceration. Then, in the gloom, she saw a human shape emerge from the shadows. It walked towards her and stopped by her bed. It looked like her husband Alec, but it was grey, like a mist. In the centre of his chest, where his ribs should be, was a hole through which she could see the opposite wall clearly. He was reaching out to her. His mouth was moving as if he was trying to speak. She strained to hear. She followed the movements of his lips, seeking to read the words that would not come. 'Sorry…' Is that what he was mouthing? 'Sorry. I'm so sorry…' She reached out, reached to touch his hand. Her eyes barely open, in that blurred state between asleep and awake, she sought to hold him again, one last time. But her fingers clutched at nothing more solid than mist and he was gone.

Ken was up early the next day and drove to the station before the school traffic clogged the roads and the roundabouts. He checked on the prisoner – she was still asleep. Her solicitor had left a message saying she'd be there by eight. That was going to be difficult. He needed to get things in motion before she arrived and took up his time. He dispatched the SOC unit to the crime scene, along with three forensics officers. The desk sergeant would contact a magistrate to obtain a search warrant. Ken knew that he needed to carry out a thorough search of Elyse's house to make sure that there was nothing amiss, even though he felt certain she was innocent of the murder. He also ensured that a bereavement counsellor was on her way.

His boss strode in five minutes before the solicitor was due. Ken walked with him to his office. 'A word, sir?'

'Come in, son, come in. Have you got the charge sheets ready for the prisoner? We need to formally charge her, or we won't be able to keep her here much longer!'

'That's why I need to speak to you, sir. I don't think she did it.'

The D.I. first looked alarmed and then smiled smugly. 'Ah! Of course, you weren't there, were you son? You should have seen it! As soon as I walked into the office where she worked – she took one look at me and blurted out a full confession! It's the look of authority, son! Scares them witless! It comes with experience, lad. One day you'll get it.'

'Yes, sir – but I don't think, when she confessed, that she was confessing to the murder. In fact, she didn't even know her husband was dead. She asked if she could phone him…'

'Oh?' The weasel face twitched with momentary concern, then settled into rodent like smugness. 'I see. She's trying to back out. It's obvious. She's thought it over and decided to retract her confession. Bloody pain. But she's got previous. And there were witnesses! They all heard it! She won't wriggle out of this!'

Ken strove to remain calm. He had to break this gently. 'It looks like she'll have a watertight alibi. She was at the office in Yeovil by eight thirty. The pathologist says he was killed between eight and nine o'clock. She couldn't have done it.'

The inspector's face was red with fury. 'Bloody pathologist! She's only just out of school! Interfering bitch! We'll get a second opinion. I'll get Doc Griffiths to take a look. He owes me a favour.'

Ken was disturbed by this and protested immediately, 'He must be eighty.'

'Bloody right. He's got the experience we need. He'll give us a better timing. Meantime, we'd better get the area searched – with a fine toothcomb! If we can find the knife and her prints are on it, we're laughing!'

Ken sighed. This wasn't going to get any better. 'I've got a search team on their way now, with forensic support. And I'm organising a house search.'

'Good lad! Let's get this business tied up!'

'But it wasn't a knife wound. Doctor Peterson found he was killed by a shotgun. She found the shell in the man's spine. She says he was killed from at least eighty yards away by someone who's a crack shot!'

The Inspector's fury was sufficient to turn the air as blue as his face as the veins swelled out on his forehead. 'Bleeding, bloody pathologists! Waste of bloody space!'

'It's true though, boss. I saw the shell! It's

gone to forensics to see if we can match it up with any on our data base.'

'This changes nothing! I'm not having the investigation wrecked by a lass just out of nappies! This is a domestic - mark my words, lad! She's still the prime suspect! We'll keep her locked up until we can pin this on her so tight Houdini couldn't get out of it! If it was a shotgun that killed him, then she must have a gun somewhere! We've just got to find the bloody thing!'

'At eighty yards, sir? Through the heart?'

'Lucky shot. Come on, lad. If we have to backtrack on this, we'll look like a set of bloody pansies!' The ground was slipping from under the inspector's feet. He had announced that the case was solved. He had enjoyed a flood of good publicity on the media. His Chief had promised him a commendation. As he blustered and swore to reassure himself that he'd been right all along, he could sense his career unravelling only a few months before a glorious retirement.

Ken was about to raise a further objection when he was interrupted by the arrival of the desk sergeant. 'Scuse, sir, but a solicitor has arrived. Wants to speak to Mrs. Bartle...'

Ken guided him away from the office, where the D.I. was gnawing his way through a ballpoint pen. Elyse's solicitor, Anita Mistry, was sitting on a chair with a brief case in her lap, looking suitably serious. She had defended Elyse two years ago, on the charge of domestic violence and grievous assault. The first covid virus lockdown had proved too much for her client to endure. Families were not allowed to leave their homes. Elyse found the confinement unbearable, locked indoors with a man she no longer loved, a man who sought to control her every movement. Eventually she had snapped under the pressure. But Anita believed that they were reconciled – that they had overcome their differences and were happy together. She was both surprised and sceptical as Ken directed her to an interview room. She stared at him, questioningly. 'What are we looking at?'

Ken paused a moment, considering how much he should reveal about the mess they were in. 'She hasn't been charged. We're holding her as a possible suspect. She's with a bereavement counsellor now, so maybe we could give them another few minutes?'

The solicitor's sharp eyes narrowed. 'Unusual, isn't it? To provide bereavement counselling for the person who did the killing?'

'Yes,' Ken admitted, 'it certainly is.'

The solicitor is sharp. She recognises something unusual, something guarded in his tone. 'There's something you're not telling me,' she probes.

Ken ponders. 'I think it can wait, See what you think when you've spoken to her. Then we'll talk again, perhaps.' More quietly, 'Keep away from the D.I. if you can. Until you're sure. He won't want to let her go.'

The solicitor stared at him, as if trying to read his mind. Then she nodded and Ken walked slowly to the cell, where the bereavement counsellor sat with Elyse. She, too, was struggling to make sense of the situation. Elyse was no ordinary prisoner.

The newly widowed woman wept quietly but managed to speak through the tears. 'He came to me. In the night. I saw him, standing there!' and she pointed to a spot by the bench in her cell.

'It's not unknown. It happens. When a loved

one is lost, many tell me that they think they see them – a ghost, perhaps – as if the lost one wants to have one last glimpse of you. When my own father died, I thought I saw him the next day, sitting on the stairs, watching me. It could just be our brains trying to cope with the loss – coming to terms with it. It rarely happens again. It's a once in a lifetime thing.'

'He spoke to me. He said he was sorry. So sorry. What did he mean? What had he done?'

The counsellor shook her head sadly. Interpreting dreams was beyond her remit. Ken was at the door. He coughed, tactfully, to attract their attention. 'Elyse. Your solicitor is here. She's waiting for you in the interview room. Are you ready to see her? Or do you want longer with Marjorie?'

Yes, she was ready. Elyse rose and the counsellor closed her notepad and gave Ken a meaningful glance. He mouthed a response, so that Elyse wouldn't hear. 'I know. Hang on a minute and I'll be back.'

He helped Elyse down the corridor. She hadn't touched her breakfast and was unsteady on her legs. Only when she was settled in the hard chair opposite her legal representative did he return to the cell. The counsellor was waiting in the doorway. She launched straight into what was on her mind. 'That woman hasn't killed anyone. She's distraught. She's lost her husband and doesn't know how or why!'

'I believe you. But the D.I. is positive she did it. His reputation rests on it. He can't back down on this one.'

'I'm giving you my professional opinion. It's inhuman to keep that poor woman in jail. She needs friends and support around her. What evidence has he got? He says she confessed? To something she clearly didn't do? Did he coerce her?'

'No, nothing like that. I think there's been a terrible misunderstanding. Look, let's leave it to her solicitor. Hopefully we can get her released within hours. Then I'll take her back home while we search the house.'

'My god!'

'I sincerely believe that it'll just be a formality. Trust me on this.'

'On your head be it. I'm going to put it on record that I am very unhappy about this.'

Ken sighed – not for the first time that day and not for the last. 'It's your right.'

Anita, the solicitor upon whom Ken was depending, was of Indian descent. She had flawless olive brown skin and dark eyes that held you in a calm steady gaze, full of reassurance. If you were her client. But rather piercing, actually, if you happened to be a police detective with a worried conscience. Ken made sure that Elyse was comfortably settled and then made a swift, tactful withdrawal.

Anita touched the fingers on Elyse's right hand, sympathetically. 'How are they treating you?'

'All right. I'm just confused.'

'Relax. Let's see if we can get you out of here. Now remember – it's just like last time. I want you to be absolutely honest with me. You must be, or I can't defend you. So tell me. What happened?'

'Nothing. I didn't do anything. They took me from work and locked me up. And then they told me that Alec…Alec…he's dead!'

Anita appraised her dispassionately. There was no trace of guilt in her. There was no need to press her. She was gazing at a truly distraught, bewildered and innocent woman who had no idea what had happened or why she was here.

'The police say that you confessed. It's been on the news. What happened? What did you say? Can you remember?'

'I didn't think! I just thought it was last time – you know? I thought he had decided to press charges after all. I thought he'd changed his mind about us! I thought…and now he's gone…oh god!'

Anita rose and put her arm around the heartbroken woman. 'They've got it all wrong. What a mess! Don't worry. We can sort this out.' She was accustomed to dealing with clients who were tearful, but Elyse was sobbing her heart out. She kept a plentiful supply of tissues in her bag and pulled out a handful, passing them to Elyse, laying a reassuring hand on her shoulder. 'Wait here.'

Anita knocked on the door of the interview room. The desk sergeant appeared and unlocked it. He found himself face to face with a grim and angry lady solicitor. 'I want to see whoever is responsible for arresting my client. I want to see him now. And I want her out of here!'

There was no way that Detective Inspector Longbottom was going to release Elyse Bartle until he legally had to. Ken knew that. The D.I. was determined to prove, right or wrong, that Elyse was guilty. Not to do so would be a humiliation. He had gone too far with this to be proved wrong. He would look ridiculous, to the press, in front of the television cameras, to the Chief Constable. And so Sergeant Jones had done the best he could. He'd left a message for his boss to tell him that the suspect's solicitor had demanded her release and now he was driving to her home. He had obtained the warrant he needed for what he suspected would be a fruitless search. He had suggested that Elyse could attend the search with them, and she was following behind with her solicitor in Anita's car.

If his boss found out that he had allowed this, he would be angry, but Ken couldn't see a problem. There was no need for her to be put in a police car for the journey. She was hardly likely to make a run for it and her solicitor would ensure that she arrived safely. It just seemed a civilised way of doing things; It was the least he could do, considering what they had put the woman through.

And anyway, Elyse had the key to the house.

They opened the door and entered. The house was deathly quiet. Nothing was disturbed. It was like coming back home after a short holiday. It made you aware of the smells of the house, scents you had not noticed while you were always there. Everything felt both familiar and strange. And still. And tidy. This did not seem like the home of someone who had set off the day before to murder her husband.

Ken sent Jenny off to search for a shotgun, or any evidence that this had once been home to a firearm. Meanwhile. Detective Sergeant Ken Jones began to earn his salary by thinking through the likely scenarios. If Elyse had not killed her husband – as seemed most likely – who did? And why? Was there someone out there who had a serious grudge against him? Was he involved, without Elyse knowing, in some shady dealing? Drugs, perhaps? Recent killings – and there were very few – in the big cities had been related to wars between rival drug gangs. But in rural Dorset? It didn't seem likely, but nothing should be ruled out at this stage. He began to search for bank statements, whilst keeping an eye open for anything suspicious, anything that might suggest that Alec was dealing in anything underhand.

No sign of bank details. The modern predilection for paperless banking was good for the planet, but a pain in the bum for good, hard-working coppers. He opened the laptop computer that lurked under a bookshelf. It was password protected. He carried it upstairs, searching for Elyse. Hopefully, she would know how to start it.

Elyse was sitting on the bed, staring at one of the two wardrobes. The doors were open. It was clearly the one which Alec had used. Jackets and trousers on hangers, shirts neatly folded, a tidy pile of pullovers, two small drawers that held pants and socks. Her face was immobile. Her eyes stared unblinking at the clothes she'd cared for, washed, ironed, folded. These were the outer garments that had clothed her husband. He would never need them again. She would never carry them, from the ironing board, upstairs to this place: never hear his thanks when he saw how she cared for him. Seeing the empty jackets, the empty suits - and knowing that his body was gone - was too much for her to bear. She was dumb with grief. The enormity of it all overwhelmed her.

Ken sat down next to her on the bed, the computer on his lap. He didn't know what to say. He had broken bad news to people before. A husband who had died in a traffic accident. A father lost in a tragedy at work. A mother, passed on from a heart attack. But, on these occasions, a female constable accompanied him. They broke the news together. He expressed his condolences in his deep, comforting voice. He registered the disbelief, the shock on the faces of those who had lost a loved one so unexpectedly. But then he was gone, leaving his junior colleague to deal with the grief. This was new to him. He was on his own with a grieving woman. And he needed her help.

'Elyse, I know this is a bad time for you, but...' She burst into floods of tears. That had not gone well. He almost put his arm around her, but stopped himself. It seemed the natural, humane way to respond, but they had suffered hours of in-house training against it. Dire warnings graphically displayed in PowerPoint after PowerPoint. The dangers of touching. The possible consequences. Misunderstandings. Inappropriate relationships. Complaints registered on the official records – or even worse.

'Elyse, I am so sorry – I need to ask you something!'

She turned to look at him. It was still early Spring, but his skin was already slightly tanned. There were flecks of green in his eyes. His brown hair was swept back, full, with just the suggestion of a wave. During the year and a half of lockdown it had grown long and a little wild, but now it was neatly trimmed. He had white even teeth, an attractive smile and a firm, Roman nose. She managed just the slightest smile. 'I'm sorry. It's just I can't believe he's gone. It's all here. Just like it was.'

Again, the urge to touch her hand, fought back. 'He's gone. Elyse, and we need to find out who did it and why. Can you tell me – is this his laptop?'

'What? Yes.'

'It's password protected. We need to open it, to find who was messaging him. Who might have had a grudge. His password, Elyse. Can you tell me what it is?'

She looked back at him blankly. She'd washed her face before leaving the cell but had no desire to brush her hair or put on any make-up. Even if she had any. She looked white and drawn, with bloodshot eyes from constant weeping. Her locks, normally her best feature, hung down unkempt and straggly. 'Can you think of a word he might have used? Your name perhaps? The name of a pet? His date of birth?'

It was no use. She began to rock to and fro. The full magnitude of what was happening was just beginning to hit her. She couldn't think clearly. Bravely, she fought back another outburst of sobs. Ken took pity. 'Don't worry, Elyse. We have people who can bypass the protection if they have to. I'll take it back with me. Is that okay?' She had no choice, but it cost nothing to be polite. Elyse nodded dumbly. 'I want to let you stay here tonight. In your home. I'll talk to your solicitor. But you must promise not to leave the village. Will you do that?' He was talking to her as if to a child, but he felt he needed to keep things simple so that she could take in what he was telling her. 'We'll want to talk to you again. Is there someone we can contact? Family? A friend? Someone who could stay with you tonight?'

There had been someone, a long time ago. A man she'd been ready to leave her husband for. Looking back on it now, it seemed so silly. She remembered the feelings as if she had been a foolish schoolgirl lost in a juvenile crush. Once upon a time she would have fallen into his arms at a time like this. But he had proved utterly fickle. He too had been swept along by the excitement of an illicit romance, but in the end the pull of home and children had been too strong for him to resist. She had learned a hard lesson. She wasn't going to be broken again.

At that moment Anita walked into the bedroom. She took in the situation with a perceptive glance from her dark brown eyes. 'She has a sister in Bournemouth. I'll get in touch. Leave her now.' She gazed sadly at the broken wreck of a woman slumped on the bed. 'The police have done enough damage, don't you think?'

9

Detective Inspector Longbottom was in a foul mood as he drove to Bishop Farthing to check on the search team. He turned on his siren and blue flashing lights as he left the A road, swinging onto the narrow winding lanes that led to the village. He was determined not to give way on the narrowest parts, where only one car could pass. A tractor driver had to screech to a halt as the car roared straight at it. The farmer cursed as he tried to back the tractor and trailer out of the way. Longbottom ignored the beauty of the hedgerows as he flashed by. The snowdrops were long gone, but the verges were bright with buttercups and dandelions, the frothy white of old man's beard and the deep purple of clover flowers. A squirrel scampered to safety as a tyre almost ran over its tail and a pheasant strutted back and forth mouthing angry complaints to the car's rear as it roared by.

He drove dangerously far into the field that led to the bluebell wood, almost grounding the car in deep, dried ruts that tractors had caused during the wet of winter. Getting out, he slammed the door shut, sending hundreds of starlings fleeing from their nests in the hedgerows. The policeman on guard snapped to attention.

'Sir!'

'Bloody village! Bloody terrible roads! Bloody farmers! Get out of my bloody way!'

'S..s..sir!' stammered the unfortunate copper, struggling to move aside and getting caught in a tangle of barbed wire. The D.I. pushed him aside and stormed up to the SOC unit leader who was directing the search. Before he could reach him, he was surrounded by reporters and hangers on who were pointing video cameras and recorders at him. He roughly pushed away a microphone that was likely to go up his nose. 'No questions! You're preventing police officers carrying out their business! Clear the area!'

'Have you solved the case, sir?'

'Have you charged the suspect yet?'

'What message do you want to send our

viewers about their safety?'

'Name, sir! Have you got a name?'

Detective Inspector Longbottom did have a name — a very rude name for interfering reporters who got in his way. He was very tempted to use it. 'Clear off! This is a designated search area! You're destroying vital evidence! I'll have you all arrested!' Never mind what this looked like on the news. He was in no mood to own up to his problems to this bunch of yoiks. And he was in no better mood when he reached the team of Scene of Crime Officers on their hands and knees, plastic body suits covering their uniforms, scouring the undergrowth round where the body had been found.

'I want every bloody inch covered with a fine toothcomb! I want proof of what went on here! Any evidence that a woman was involved — you hear me? What's turned up so far, eh?'

The nervous officer said nothing, but presented his superior with a box containing an assortment of small plastic evidence bags. The D.I. rifled through it. A broken comb, a used condom, one heel from a hobnailed boot, the chewed half of a dog toy and a potato crisp wrapper. The Detective Inspector threw these back into the box and swung away. He was determined that he was right. The woman he'd arrested was so clearly guilty, had so obviously broken down with guilt when he accosted her, that he refused to admit that there could be any mistake. He was not a man to trust the verdict of a rooky pathologist over his own tried and trusted instincts. He barked into his phone. He wanted the key team members back at base immediately. He needed to plan the investigation in order to get quick results.

But as the detectives drove back to base, the tendrils of the news media were even then worming their way into the homes of the villagers. No less a personage than Bill Stott, the (sour) cream of the reporting staff of the most popular, red-topped tabloid, knocked on door after door. He had many scoops to his name. He was the one with his camera at the ready when a minor celebrity had an unfortunate (and prearranged) mishap with her bikini top. She claimed it was an accident, and it got her much needed publicity when her cleavage was spread across the front page. It was Bill Stott's notebook that recorded the confessions of a footballer's wife. She told a steamy story of her husband's infidelity, with her sister, in a B&B in Bognor. It had led to a libel case, true, but it did wonders for sales as it ran for weeks. And it was this same Bill Stott who now prowled the streets of Bishop Farthing, determined to find scandal behind the death in the woods.

Those of you familiar with the village and its inhabitants will draw in a breath when I tell you that the first house he called at was the home of Mrs Simpkins. Not for nothing had she earned the nickname of the Merry Widow.

'Good morning. I wonder if I could trouble you for a few minutes of your time? I'm a reporter working for…'

'No trouble at all! Come in! Come in!' The widow bustled him into her parlour, whilst surreptitiously undoing another button on her housecoat to reveal even more of her ample bust.

'Can I get you a drink?'

'Tea – would be nice…'

'I was just getting myself a gin and orange. I'll do one for you.'

'It's a bit early…'

'Nonsense. Now sit here next to me. I know all the local gossip. You've come to the right place!'

'Thank you, Mrs?'

'Mrs. Simkins. Not married, though. Widowed. I've been without for three – nearly four – years now. Freda, though. You must call me Freda!' It seemed to the doughty reporter that she was leaning against him rather more than was strictly necessary.

'Now Mrs…Freda, this body in the wood?'

'Terrible, isn't it? Nothing like this ever happened here before! But it makes you think, doesn't it? And me – all alone in the house!'

'Ah - so you think the killer may be at large? Maybe someone local?'

'My hubby, bless his heart, I always felt safe with him around. He kept a golf club under the bed. Sometimes he'd slap me on the bum with it. Only gently, of course. Called it fore - play, he did. Oh, he made me laugh!'

'Now Freda, what's the word on the street? Someone must know the name…'

Freda didn't seem to be interested in the

killing any more. Her face was flushed. 'But the last couple of years, he was ill, you see. Didn't have it in him, if you get my meaning.' She leant over and placed her hand on the reporter's knee. 'He knew he wasn't giving me what I wanted. I'm a woman with, well, warm feelings, you see.' She squeezed her hand around his thigh. He squirmed a little.

He tried to get her back on track. 'Mrs Simpkins, I'm sorry but if you can't give me what I need…'

'Oh, but I can dear! That's what I'm telling you! You see, Mr Simpkins, bless his heart, spoke to me. While I was filling his hot water bottle one night. He said, Freda, he said. I know you're a woman with needs. A woman's needs. And if I can't give you what you want, then I won't mind. He wouldn't mind, you see. He said so. When I got back and was sorting out his drip. If you can get it someplace else, he said. Oh, I can hear him now. He was far gone, of course. And with the drugs and all. But he whispered in my ear clear as day.' One of her buxom breasts was now pressing against his arm. She rubbed it against him, suggestively. 'If there's someone else who can do it for you…'

Bill got, unsteadily, to his feet. 'Sorry, Mrs. Simpkins but I've got my job to do…'

'But you haven't finished your drink!'

'Later perhaps…another time…'

The widow understood. He needed to get the story for his paper. But once he had done, he could call back. Would come back. After all, she had so much to offer. She would help him. 'Oh, all right. You'd better call at that Beth woman's house. Across the road. She found the body…'

Ah, thank you. That house there? Thank you!'

'Don't mention it. When you've finished, I'll be here! I'll keep your drink on ice!' She grabbed his jacket and whispered hotly in his ear. 'But everything else will be hot, get my meaning?'

He did. And he fled.

He pushed open the gate to Beth's garden. It swung uncertainly on its hinges, as if someone heavy had, in the past, knocked into it. The path was lined with geraniums that cascaded blue flowers onto the flagstones. He trod carefully so as not to squash any of them. Best not to annoy the public before questioning them. He ignored the towering spikes of delphiniums and lupins and headed for the front door. The knocker was in the shape of a heart. Surely not another of them, he thought to himself. All the inhabitants of Bishop Farthing can't be sex mad, can they? He tapped once and there was the sound of a bolt drawing back. Then the door opened a couple of inches, held back on a chain. A pair of pretty, brown eyes squinted at him through the gap. Beth was taking no chances, with a murderer possibly on the loose.

'Good morning, madam. I'm calling on the recommendation of your neighbour, Mrs. Simpkins.'

He looked for a positive response. None came. It seemed that the mention of Mrs. Simpkins was not the key to gaining this woman's trust. 'She said that you may be able to help me. I understand that you were the one who found the body?' Still no response. The two brown eyes stared unblinking, unmoved, at him – through him. 'I wonder if I might come in?' Obviously not. He continued as though he hadn't noticed the snub. 'I was hoping for a statement from you. About what you saw. What you did? Could I start with your name?'

At last, a response. The eyes fluttered slightly. Then, from somewhere beneath them, a voice. Calm but steady. Calm but determined. Calm – but hostile. 'What paper are you from?'

Bill's heart sank. Only one type of person would ask a question like that. Ninety-five per cent of the population, in his experience, are thrilled to speak to a reporter. They want their names in the paper. It is their chance of five minutes of fame. It is the same instinct for public acknowledgement and glory that leads otherwise sensible people to volunteer to go on 'Escape to the Country' when they haven't sold their home. Or to make fools of themselves on 'Bargain Hunt'. Or to humiliate themselves publicly on the 'Jeremy Kyle Show' before it was closed down by do-gooders and killjoys.

Just his luck that this was a person who harboured unjustified antipathy to his type of tabloid newspaper. He recognised her type at once. A Guardian reader. Typical - the one person who could give him the scoop he needed was one who wasted her time reading a paper that dealt only with facts and educated opinions, when it was clear from the mass demand for his sheet that what the customers really yearned for was scandal and tittle tattle.

He made one final attempt to break through. 'We've been known to pay handsomely for exclusives. We could be talking a four figure sum…'

As the door slammed shut, he distinctly heard a woman's voice tell him to 'Sod off!'

'Very ladylike,' he muttered as he turned to walk back down the path, deliberately crushing several flower heads as he did so. Exiting through the uneven gate, his eye was caught by a movement at the upstairs window of Mrs. Simpkins' cottage. The said lady was waving to him, coquettishly. Another button of her housecoat seemed to have come undone. Bill Stott swung away and walked briskly in the opposite direction. All was not lost. True, he had not gained the interview that he craved. But he could always fall back on the ruse that all tabloid reporters use when news is thin on the ground. Make something up.

While Bill Stott was searching Bishop Farthing, in vain, for a pub where he could enjoy a lunchtime drink, on expenses, while he wrote his story, the team was assembling at headquarters. Jenny had pinned a row of pictures onto a large whiteboard. This system of displaying visual clues to a crime on a board for everyone to gaze at — as if staring at them long enough would reveal the answer — was popularised on many television crime series. It was a way for the programme makers to keep the main points of the plot in front of viewers' eyes in case they forgot what they were watching and why. It proved so popular that real police forces began to use it. Sales of white boards rose considerably.

Detective Inspector Cyril Longbottom stared at the row of photographs, muttering as he did so at the ones of the gunshot wound that had so complicated his line of enquiry. He snorted and then turned to face his eager group of detectives facing him in the open plan office. 'Right!' he barked. 'Listen up!'

He walked across to the picture board and stabbed a crooked finger aggressively at the mug shot of Elyse Bartle. 'Still our chief suspect!' He looked accusingly at Ken Jones, still not forgiven for allowing her release. 'She has previous. Charged with causing grievous bodily harm to her husband in 2020. Never came to court because, when he recovered, he refused to press charges. Silly sod. We have to suspect that she finally succeeded. Motive? It could be financial. We'll need to check insurance records and bank accounts. Geoff? You'll cover that!'

'Yes, boss.' Geoff had the sort of face you could trust in a crisis. He had trained as a plumber before he joined the force, so he was more comfortable than most dipping into the sewage of financial excrement.

'Could be she was involved with another man and this was her way of clearing the way. Jenny – check through her phone records and look for anything suspicious!'

'Started already, boss! Nothing suspicious in the past week – only calls for business or to her husband.'

'Good work. Keep at it. And remember – the other man could be a work colleague!' Jenny nodded and glanced sadly at Ken, but he was too occupied to notice. He was second in command and he resented the implication that he'd been in error.

'We should remember, sir, that the victim

was struck with a gunshot wound at eighty yards. There's no sign of a weapon at the house nor any evidence that there has ever been one.'

The Detective Inspector smirked in a way that represented his much greater experience and knowledge. 'Not every domestic is straightforward, lad. When you've seen all the cases I have, you'll be less gullible! She didn't have to shoot him herself, did she?' With a note of triumph: 'She could have got her fancy man to shoot him! Or hired a hitman! What would it cost, eh? Five grand? And she could have him insured for millions!'

Ken was not going to be put down in public that easily. 'She was desolate, sir. Not like a woman who's just got what she wanted. She's barely stopped crying since I broke the news to her.'

'Don't be taken in by a pretty face, son!'

Jenny looked down, embarrassed, but no-one noticed. They were all concentrating on this exchange between the two senior members of the team. It seemed at face value to be of little import – but they all knew that a potential earthquake was rumbling beneath the surface.

'An act, lad! Women are good at it! She'll be behind this, mark my words. We just need to find the proof!'

10

nnette lay in bed, trembling even though the weather was warm. She pulled her nightdress down over her knees. Dennis was snoring. Her distress had not disturbed him. Little did nowadays, she thought with a slight touch of bitterness. Annette had woken from a bad dream. She had been at the edge of a wide meadow, yellow with buttercups. There was a large house in the distance, but she couldn't recognise it. At the other side of the field a woman was screaming. She was trying to tell Annette something, but it was impossible to understand her. She didn't seem to be calling out in English. It was vital that she was heard. Annette knew that she had to understand and help her, but try as she might, she couldn't.

Annette had dreams like this before. Nine months before her son was born, she had a premonition that a child was on his way. Half asleep she had a vague impression that there was

– in the corner of the room – something…was it a cot? Painted white with nursery rhyme scenes on the ends? But when she shook her head and cleared her sight, there was nothing. Just a chest of drawers and the chair she left her clothes on, ready for the morning. A year later, with a white cot next to her bed, she remembered the dream and wondered. She curled up against Dennis, His back was warm and comfortable. She drifted off to sleep again. But the next morning she couldn't get the image of the screaming woman out of her mind.

There had been other times. During the first lockdown. When the virus struck. Martha, the spinster across the road, the one who was so steeped in religious dogma that she never noticed the wonder and beauty that God had spread around her for us all to enjoy, had gone missing. No-one had seen her. Her house was closed up, the curtains drawn. Some said she must have gone away – on a retreat, perhaps. Others worried that she had passed away, was lying dead in the house, and were too afraid to check on her. Annette alone felt that she was there – still alive but in need of help. It was only Annette who had the courage to drag her husband across, to check the door, to find it unlocked, to go up the stairs. It was Annette who opened her bedroom door and found her, lying on her bed, arms crossed over her breast, breathing shallowly. She'd looked like a statue on a tomb in Bishop Farthing's church.

Certain that the pandemic marked the second coming, Martha was waiting to meet her God, confident that she alone of all her neighbours would be a chosen one, invited to enter his Kingdom. It was Annette who coaxed some soup between her lips and eventually convinced her that this was not yet the time.

When Annette's father had lain, desperately ill, in their front room, an oxygen cylinder by his bed, it was Annette who saw the shadow. It waited patiently by the mantelpiece, alongside the plaster dogs and the two silver candlesticks that her mother polished every week but never lit.

Under the black marble clock that ticked away the seconds, minutes, hours, days…offering up one solemn, echoing chime every hour – it lurked, uncomplaining, biding its time. Then, early one morning, the young Annette had seen the shadow outside her bedroom window. It had lingered for a moment there, as if calling goodbye to her, and then it was gone. And the little girl knew that she should stay upstairs, away from the adult grief that broke around her. She knew that he had loved her. That he had called to her. That he was sorry to leave her and had made one last farewell.

Other women in the village recognised that Annette had the sight. If they had a form to fill in, they would check with her that they had done it correctly. If seeds were not growing as they should, they would ask her advice. Annette had little knowledge of horticulture, but she would pause and think. When an answer came to her it was usually correct. Pets were sometimes carried to her and she would tell the worried owner whether a vet visit was required, or if money could be saved and the creature would recover without.

Annette had a sense, then, that something was wrong and that meant that she was required to act on it. She did not know who the woman was, where she lived or why she was crying out to her. But she had to act. But who to tell? Because Annette also had a good instinct about people. Although this didn't extend to her choice of husband. Maybe she'd accepted his proposal when her gifts were at a low ebb. Dennis wasn't that bad, though, taken all in all.

But the Detective Inspector in charge of the enquiry? She had serious doubts. Annette knew a non-believer when she met one. He would laugh her off as a silly woman – a crackpot. She knew better than to waste her talents on such as him. There were others – ones she felt she could trust.

Annette left the comfort of her home to walk toward the wood. She was following an instinct. She could not have explained her actions if anyone had asked. She just knew that she had to go. Across the field, past the police cars lined up on the grass, round the police tape marking off the search area. From a safe distance she watched the line of men on their hands and knees scouring their way through the brambles, nettles, tall grass and bluebells that covered the ground. It seemed to her that there was something pointless and dull about their work. She moved away, deeper into the wood. She reached the wire fence that marked the edge, spattered with random hedgerow and the occasional small rowan tree. On the other side was a further meadow, where she had on occasion seen deer racing from side to side, light and graceful on their feet. Her attention was drawn to a break in the fence, where a post had split and now leaned at a crazy angle. Next to it, a patch of undergrowth had been flattened. She instinctively knew that someone had been there, furiously angry, determined to inflict hurt on someone. It was outside the search area. She dismissed it from her mind.

Moving closer to the blue tape, she caught the attention of a female officer. She was wiping the sweat from her brow. The effort of crawling through the tangled growth on the forest floor was beginning to get to her, particularly as it had so far been fruitless. Annette beckoned her. 'I need to talk to someone.'

'You've got some information?'

'I'm not sure. It may be nothing.'

'Well, ma'am, we don't ignore anything that may be helpful, even if it seems very minor. Everything is shared and recorded. You just never know.'

'Shall I tell you?'

'I'm just a SOCO, ma'am.' Annette looked

confused. The woman wrapped in plastic explained: 'A scene of crime officer. You need to talk to one of the detectives. There's a big team on the case.'

'That's all right.' Then, hesitantly, 'I'd rather not speak with the man leading it. He might think I'm just wasting his time.'

The woman gave her a critical stare. Was she a reliable and useful source? Probably not. But she shared her doubts about Detective Inspector Longbottom. She, too, kept out of his way as much as she could. 'I'll put you in touch with others on the team, ma'am.' She switched on her phone. 'Can you get me Detective Sergeant Jones, please. Or D.C. Jenny Grace?'

While the operator tried to locate them, the woman police officer stretched her arms and straightened her back. Whatever came of this, at least it meant that she could stand upright for a few minutes and ease some of the pain in her thigh muscles. 'They're searching for them now, love. Give me your name and address and they'll be in touch, I'm sure.'

Annette did so and then ventured further round the tape barrier to a part of the wood she'd never visited before. She was following the broken, haphazard fence that marked the boundary. Suddenly she stopped short. There, through a break in the fence she saw it. Across the fields, some distance away. It was the large house she'd seen in her dream.

Doctor Sheila Peterson pushed her plate away and looked round the pub in despair. She had agreed to this lunch date so that she could talk seriously to Harold about their relationship. She was increasingly certain that it was wrong for her, but ending it was proving problematical. The surroundings, however, were unhelpful. For one thing there was too much noise. A wallpaper of music played, too loudly, from hidden speakers — one just above their heads. Other diners and drinkers were conversing stridently all around her. To have any sort of conversation would mean shouting. The sentiments she needed to convey were best not called out aloud in public. In desperation, she suggested that they get in one of the cars and drive somewhere quieter. Harold jumped at the idea.

He led her to his BMW and it was obvious that he knew a suitable spot. He drove swiftly to a small side road and then to a clearing with picnic tables in Wareham forest. There were two other cars parked there, but they were a distance away.

It immediately became clear that Harold had misunderstood when she made the suggestion that they needed to be alone. He got out of the car and opened the passenger door. He then got in the rear and waited expectantly for her to join him. She had no choice. Either she got onto the back seat with him, or stood alone at the side of the car. Accepting the inevitable, she sat next to him, but left her door slightly ajar, hoping that this would indicate that she wanted to talk, not have sex. But he was not to be swayed from his objective.

He kissed her by her ear, on her neck. She wasn't offering her lips, still hoping to discourage him, to convey her reluctance. She failed. One of his hands caressed her breasts and then slipped to her knees. It began to move up under her skirt. She recognised his urgent need for her and decided to submit. One last time and then, in the calm that follows sexual release, she would break the news to him. She wouldn't meet him again like this. Their relationship must become platonic. Professional. She was grateful for all he had done for her, but it was time for her to seek her independence.

Still nibbling at her neck, he undid his belt. She helped him to release himself and then spread her legs, pulling her underwear aside. He began to mount her. It was clumsy, uncomfortable. She turned her head away from him, trying to shrug herself into a more relaxed position. It was then she saw him.

A man was approaching the car. He was in his forties, with dark unkempt hair. His trousers were open at the front, and he was exposing himself. Startled, she looked at the other cars. Next to one of them – she had not noticed before – a couple were peering in, watching the action inside. The woman was masturbating her friend as they peered in at the antics of the car's occupants. Furious, she pushed her right hand down between her legs and used her left to push at Harold with all the strength she could muster.

'How could you bring me to a place like this? You knew, didn't you?'

'Calm down! They're just doggers!'

'I know what they are! It's disgusting!'

'There's no harm in it. It makes a change.

129

Adds a bit of spice…'

'Not for me! It's filthy! I'm not here to perform for these perverts!' Then realisation dawned. 'You come here, don't you! That's how you knew to come here!'

'Not that much. Now and again. Loosen up. Don't be such a prig. The ones who come here do it because they want people to watch. It gives them a bit of a turn on.'

'Get me out of here!' She felt sick, suddenly. 'I mean it.'

In stony silence they drove back to the pub car park and she got out of his car without speaking to him. She slammed the passenger door shut and strode across to her own car. All she wanted now was to get away from him. To end it.

11

Ken had just been passed the victim's financial details when his phone rang. He recognised Sheila's number.

'Hi Sheila, okay?'

'Yeh – just wondering. Are you doing anything tonight?'

'Me? No.'

'I could do with some good company. Someone to restore my faith in men.'

'And you thought of me? You sure?'

'I'll take my chance. Would you like to come round tonight? For supper?'

'Yes, thank you, I would.'

'Half seven? Spagbol all right?'

'My favourite.'

'Sure. See you then. Half seven.'

'Bye!'

'Bye.'

He looked up. Jenny was standing next to him with another sheet of bank statements. 'Was that the pathologist lady?'

Ken paused, surprised. 'Yes. Sheila Peterson.'

'She's nice, isn't she? Wish I had her legs.'

Ken didn't know what to say. 'Yes. No. You're…' He was saved by the phone ringing again. This time it was a member of the SOC unit in Bishop Farthing wood.

'Sorry – I'd better take this. What? Hi! How's it going? Nothing at all? Well, we had to try…Okay, give me her address. I'll try to call in later today. Thanks!' By the time he put the phone down, Jenny was gone.

She stared at the computer screen, unable to concentrate on what was displayed. Jenny did not understand why some people are noticed, make an impression, and some not. She was efficient in her job. Whatever she was asked to produce, she could normally find within minutes – a few hours at the most. It seemed to her that it was taken for granted that she would use her internet skills to find the mundane details that the team needed. She knew that she was bright, that she had more to give if it was asked of her. But she was given the leads to follow that were unlikely to lead anywhere – the members of the public to interview who were of least interest to the investigation.

She was the kind of girl who was always going to be the bridesmaid. Jenny was slightly dumpy (but in much better shape than her self-image led her to believe) and no amount of dieting could make her slender, it seemed. Her hair was jet black and bleaching it just left it looking false. She had gone blonde once in the sixth form, knowing that blondes catch men's eyes and, apparently, have more fun. It didn't suit her complexion. It looked silly and she'd been mocked by her school friends. She lived an agony of humiliation and embarrassment until she could grow it out.

She thought again of last year's Christmas get together with the team. She already knew their boss had little respect for her – or for any woman in truth. At one point, when they were singing scurrilous versions of Christmas carols and he had found himself standing next to her, he had touched her bottom. She had moved quickly away from him. Jenny knew that she should have made an official complaint, reported it. But it would have been his word against hers and certainly wouldn't have helped her career.

Then she had shared a taxi home with Ken. Ken was steady and always polite to her. Jenny never expected her offer to stay the night would be accepted, but it was. She'd had one partner before – but a boy compared with Ken.

She was tipsy but the sex was great. When he left in the morning – it wasn't a workday – she had lain in bed for hours remembering the touch of him, the muscle on his arms, the stubble on his face. The kindness in his eyes, his gentleness. She had fantasised about a future together. How she would cook for him, cuddle up with him at night, love him. But there'd been no follow up for her. When they met again, it was as if nothing had happened.

She knew, as did the rest of the team, that it was Ken who was the brains on the team. She recognised that he had to be deferential to Longbottom – he was in charge after all. But it was Ken who came up with the theories, the good ideas. But this case wasn't going well. The D.I. was undermining him, convinced, despite all the evidence to the contrary, that he was right.

She sent a request to the insurance data base for details of any policies on Alec Bartle and then noticed Ken getting to his feet and picking up his jacket from the back of his chair. She jumped in immediately. 'Are you going to an interview, sarge?'

'Yep. A woman says she has some information. Probably nothing, but best to check it out.'

'Shall I come with you? If it's a female witness?'

This made sense. Ken knew that these days it was best to cover your back. 'Yes – if you don't mind.'

'No prob, sarge!'

Ken drove and Jenny was happy to sit in silence as they made their way to Bishop Farthing. She knew he had a date that night. She suspected that it was with the very attractive new pathologist. She had sensed something developing between them. But it was good just to be out with Ken, doing something more interesting than analysing files on the computer. She felt at peace as they sped along the narrow country lanes, between the high hedges, slowing for pheasants on the road, swerving to avoid hedgehogs. Beneath the hedges was a riot of wildflowers. It was so quiet. So beautiful. Difficult to believe anything wicked could happen in these idyllic surroundings.

The village of Bishop Farthing consists of perhaps a hundred dwellings, spread out over several square miles of Dorset countryside. It has no defined village centre. It is a scattering of hamlets, joined together by a maze of twisting, narrow lanes. There are no footpaths, No streetlights. The only facilities a small village hall; a shop two or three miles away from many of the homes; and the church of St Egladine with its small school, so far from the homes that almost all the children are brought there by car.

Ken had begun to know his way around and anyway Orchard Lane, where Annette lives, is one of the main lanes through the village. There was still some delay because none of the houses have numbers. Spotting and deciphering all the names took time, but, eventually, they successfully located Laurel Cottage. There was a contractor's van parked outside. Dennis had undertaken an ill-advised DIY project during the pandemic lockdown that had almost brought the house down on his family's heads. Restoration work was still ongoing.

They had to park in front of Martha's cottage and Jenny, remembering this lady's heavy leather-bound Bible and her dire warnings of the second coming, kept her face pointed away in case the mad woman recognised her and ran out waving copies of The Watchtower. She almost skipped behind Ken as he walked to Annette's front door, so pleased to be with him and involved in some practical detective work.

Annette shouted for them to come in and asked them to sit in the front room while she finished changing a nappy. This was a practicality, Jenny mused, that had never cropped up in any of the police series she had watched on television before joining the force, Ken asked her to take notes, once the interview got underway, and she readily agreed.

Bishop Farthing is a very old settlement, listed in the Domesday Book from 1086 A.D. It consists of a scattering of old, thatched cottages built mainly of stone or cob and full of character, boasting low beams, inglenook fireplaces, sloping floors and single glazed windows that the owners are not allowed to replace. More modern buildings have sprung up between them: substantial Georgian farmhouses and more modern redbrick semidetached dwellings, some of which were built by the council to house local, agricultural workers. Only here and there are many of these grouped together. Generally, they are separated by small scatterings of woodland or farmer's fields. And so, although Elyse lived in the same village as Annette, her home was almost a mile from Orchard Lane, where Ken and Jenny patiently waited, the faint smell of baby poo tickling their nostrils.

The family liaison officer had just left. She had been some comfort to Elyse. She had explained carefully how she should go about registering the death of her husband, how to contact the insurance companies, how to begin to put her life back together and plan for the future. Some useful leaflets the officer left scattered across the coffee table might be handy, because Elyse had nodded and made affirmative noises during the talk, but had, in truth, taken little of it in

She had suggested that Elyse might leave home for a few days and move in with her mother or her sister. It would help to share the grieving. She'd be less alone in her sorrow. Elyse said that she would consider it, but at this moment didn't want someone fussing over her.

She stared at the room. How could everything still look the same after what had happened? There was the magazine Alec had been reading only two days ago. In the kitchen, the mug he always used was still on the draining board. His clothes from the day before he went missing were in the washing basket. She stared at them in a daze. What should she do? Wash them? Throw them? Her instinct was to clean them and put them away in his wardrobe, but the rational part of her, functioning only spasmodically, told her to dispose of them. But her overwhelming sensation was that the house was unchanged, as if waiting patiently for him to return, to greet her, peck her cheek and continue just where he left off. But the house was not the same. It was echoey, empty, lonely. She curled up on the sofa and wept.

The business with the nappy concluded satisfactorily, Annette emerged with baby under one arm and smiled apologetically. 'Sorry about that!'

'No problem! I suppose I'll have to get used to doing it one day!' Ken joked. Jenny stared at him steadily. Would he? Would she?

'One of the search team contacted me saying that you thought you had some information that could help with the enquiry.' Annette didn't reply. She gave him a doubtful look. Ken persisted, 'No matter how small. Sometimes it's the tiny details that people remember that proves to be the key to unlocking the case.' She still looked hesitant. 'No need to be nervous. We'll follow anything up you tell us.'

Annette sat down, baby on her knee. She considered this. She considered Ken. Was he someone who would have any understanding of a woman's intuition? She decided to play safe. 'I saw something. Just beyond where you'd put the blue tape. It was probably nothing – just trampled ground…'

'Could you take us to it?'

'I think so.' Annette stood, realised she was holding the baby and felt a little foolish. Jenny understood what was troubling her.

'If the going gets a little rough, I can help with the baby.'

'Thank you. There's no-one I can leave him with.'

'No problem!' Jenny couldn't see any harm in showing Ken that she was adept with babies.

There was a buggy for the infant so Jenny had no more to do than help Annette steer it safely over the bumpy bits as they entered the field. Jenny wasn't making the good impression she had hoped. Annette led the four of them to the trampled ground that she had discovered, and here Jenny was able to lift the child and carry him – it was impossible terrain for a baby buggy. Annette was wondering if she could tell them of her dream, of the screaming woman, as Ken went down on his knees to examine the ground.

'Yes. It's around eighty-five yards from

where the body fell. The D.I.'s instructions to the search team were too precise I think.' He stared at the perimeter tape, which had come just short of the spot where they stood. Determinedly, he rose and pulled the tape to cover the new site. Then he caught a glimpse of something metallic in the grass. 'Two shotgun cartridges. So two shots were fired – probably a double barrelled gun. The second shot could have passed hundreds of feet beyond him. I doubt we'll ever find it.' He squinted across the woodland. 'Yes, this is in line with where the body lay before it was moved. Thank you, Annette. I'll get someone down here to do a thorough search.'

She reached to take the baby from Jenny. As she did so, she whispered, 'There's something else. Could I tell you? I don't think a man would believe me.'

Jenny drew her aside. 'Sergeant Jones is nothing if not a good listener. It's worth giving him a try if you think it's relevant to the case.'

'I don't know. I don't know what it means.'

Jenny smiled as a plan formed in her mind. She turned to Ken. 'Can you hold this a moment

please, Ken? We just need a minute together!'
And to the detective's surprise, he was passed
the baby and Annette led Jenny away to the
boundary of the wood.

'I see things sometimes. Things that aren't
there. But they happen. I know it sounds
strange.'

It did. But Jenny had nothing better to do.
And when she glanced behind and saw Ken
looking confused and embarrassed as he tried to
work out which way up to hold the child, a few
more minutes with Annette seemed an amusing
option. Jenny was, however, a rational person
and would prove difficult to convince.

Annette pointed to a break in the fence. 'It
was over there. I saw her. She was screaming…'

'When? When was it?'

'Last night. It was a dream I suppose. But it
seemed real. There was a big house behind her!'

Jenny waved for Ken to come over. This
sounded too weird to be true to Jenny's rational
mind, but it was her duty to pass on anything
that could be a clue, no matter how unlikely. She
relieved him of the baby. 'Annette says she saw
a woman screaming. By the gap in the fence over

there.' They walked towards it, their ankles brushing against brambles and nettles. The route they followed was a path, but it was obvious that it was used only rarely. They came to a halt by the place where two of the cracked, ancient fence posts were leaning at a crazy angle and the wire was trampled down. It was an unofficial way into the wood from the large estate that stretched beyond.

Ken turned to Annette. 'When did you see her?'

Jenny jumped in to clear any misunderstandings. 'It was in a dream, sarge. She has the sight you see. She sees things...' Here she winked at Ken to show that she wasn't taken in, 'And they happen. Come true. Sometimes!'

Ken smiled. 'Well, we've got to consider every possible lead. Who knows, there could be a woman at the back of this somewhere.' He was prepared to play along. 'But you said she was screaming?'

Annette livened, thinking that she was being taken seriously. 'Screaming, yes. Trying to tell me something. She was screaming at me!'

'What did she say? Could you make it out?

Any of the words?'

Annette looked crestfallen. 'It was foreign. It wasn't in English. I couldn't understand any of it!' It was now turn for Ken to wink at Jenny. 'Well, it could be useful. We'll make a note. But this trampled ground you've found – that's a real help!' Before she could reply, Ken's phone rang. 'Hi Sheila. Okay, we'll bring her in.' He sighed and turned to the two women. 'Sorry, Annette, we've got to leave you.' Jenny passed the baby to her. Ken filled her in, 'The boss wants Elyse to go to the mortuary. She hasn't identified the body yet. And we can't go public with the name until she does. The press are getting on the case. He needs something to tell them, I suppose.'

12

etective Inspector Longbottom's foul mood was getting fouler by the minute. He had Jenny's report from the insurance data base clutched tightly in his fist. But it was a rookie detective constable who was suffering his blistering stare, 'I want these bleeding insurance details checked again! She had <u>some</u> bloody reason to kill him and I need it found and now! Check these bleeding files again!'

'Yes boss! Right away, boss!' And he turned back to his computer screen, knowing it was hopeless and wishing insurance policies could be invented. All he had found so far was the one standard mortgage protection policy Jenny had already identified, which would give Elyse no more than the house. It was something, but hardly enough to have someone murdered for.

Then the phone rang in his office. And the

very bad situation got a little worse. 'Longbottom...Oh, hello Chief...We had to release her. Sir – bloody awkward solicitor...we just didn't have enough to charge her yet...We're working on it...I'm a hundred percent confident that we're within hours of getting this tied up...Not identified formally yet, no sir...Well it seemed all settled yesterday, but we're getting it done this afternoon and then we'll release it to the press and ask for help from the public. We'll have it all tied up by tomorrow morning, chief, guaranteed!'

He crashed the phone down and stormed to his office door. He slammed his fist against the glass and fired words like bazooka shells at the three members of his team who had not yet found a good excuse to leave the office. 'I want some bloody reason to put that woman behind bars that's bleeding solicitor-proof – or you'll be out of here and walking the bloody streets as community bleeding coppers this time tomorra!' Three heads dipped down and three sets of eyes began again a hopeless search of the internet for information that wasn't there.

Ken and Jenny drove the short distance to Elyse's home in silence. This was one of the worst tasks that any police officer has to face. It was clear immediately that Elyse was still very distressed. Her eyes were red and her hair unbrushed, her face pale and drawn. She offered them a cup of tea and Jenny went with her into the kitchen to keep her company. Elyse pulled three mugs from a wall cupboard and filled the kettle. She dropped the tea bags in, still keeping herself together. However, when Jenny touched her arm and whispered, 'How are you coping, Elyse?' the poor woman burst into tears. Up to now, she had been stunned by the shock of the sudden and unexpected loss of her husband. At first it had seemed a tragic accident. She'd imagined it as a traffic accident. But of course, it wasn't.

For the past hour, she'd been dwelling on what had happened, without even knowing that he had been shot. All she knew was that he had been found dead in the wood. And it didn't make any sense. Who could have done it and why?

'I don't…don't understand…Who would want to? To hurt him?' Elyse stammered. She still couldn't bring herself to say 'kill', still didn't want to believe it. 'Can I tell you something?

Something he said…'

Jenny was instantly alert. 'Of course. Of course. Anything. When was this? What did he say?' The detective in her knew that whatever it was, it could be important. It was obviously something unusual, something that she remembered and was troubling her. Once Elyse began, though, her heart sank, and she began to wonder if all the inhabitants of Bishop Farthing were slightly deranged.

'He came to me. When I was at the station…in the cell. That night. He spoke to me!' Elyse's eyes filled with tears.

'Like a ghost?'

'He came from nowhere. Just appeared. He spoke to me…'

Jenny was far from sure that Ken would want to know this. She had no idea of his views on the supernatural but suspected he would be as circumspect as she. 'He spoke to you – what did he say? Do you remember?'

Elyse did. 'He said sorry. He said he was so, so sorry.'

Jenny played along. 'For what? Sorry for

what?'

Elyse found it difficult to speak. 'I...I don't know... He just said that and then he was ...gone!'

There was a moment of silence, of reflection, as Jenny took in the implications of this. Then, 'Was there something he was involved in, with someone perhaps, something that he shouldn't have been doing, that might have led someone to kill him?'

Elyse looked blank. 'I don't know. There could have been...'

This gave Jenny reason to call Ken over. She passed him his tea and brought him up to date. His brow furrowed a moment and then he squeezed Elyse's arm reassuringly. 'We need to find a motive for someone to do this. Once we have a motive, we'll be closer to nailing the killer. It could be there'll be things on his computer that will help us, but we haven't been able to open it yet. Think Elyse, was there anything, anything at all, that was different about the way he was behaving? Anything that seemed to be worrying him?' Elyse shook her head. Ken gave her a moment to consider this, then, 'Did his behaviour change? Was he doing anything, anything at all, that was slightly unusual or out of character?'

Elyse was lost. Ken tried to help her. 'What about this morning walk to the wood? Did he do that every morning? Would he have time before work?'

Elyse didn't know. 'I always left before him. He always cleared the breakfast things and then left. I didn't know he went to the wood. I don't know why he would.'

Jenny remembered Annette's strange dream. It was probably nothing to do with this, but – 'Could there have been someone he was going to meet?' Jenny wasn't sure how to ask, but she knew she had to. 'Think about the last few weeks. I know this is a terrible thing to suggest but we have to consider all the options: could there have been another woman?'

Elyse gave her a startled glance. 'Alec? You mean Alec? He was an accountant! He builds model kits! He's got a train set!'

Ken and Jenny exchanged amused smiles. 'They're waiting for us, Elyse. They 'd like you to identify – to confirm that it's Alec – are you up to it?' She nodded dumbly.

It was fortunate that Ken let Jenny drive the twenty miles to the mortuary. Halfway, he received a call from the Chief Constable.

'A quick word, sergeant. I've had a memorandum from the photographer on the Bartle case. He's concerned that the body was moved before the pathologist arrived.'

'Sir. The D.I. believed that the man had collapsed, sir. There was no reason to suspect that an offence had been committed.'

'Possibly not, sergeant. But were you happy with the D.I.'s decision?'

'It's normal, sir, to leave the body in position until the pathologist has arrived and inspected it.'

'Quite so, sergeant. And I understand that the initial suspect has been released and is no longer under investigation?'

This sounded like trouble. Ken knew that this case had been handled badly, but he still felt loyalty to his boss. 'She has a sound alibi, sir. for the day and time of the killing. We've checked it out and confirmed it.'

'I hardly need to tell you how embarrassing this is, sergeant. The D.I. went public with a suspect in custody and the crime all but solved. Now we'll have to backtrack. We'll look at best presumptive and at worst incompetent.'

There was little that Ken could say. 'Sir.'

'We need a fresh approach on this, sergeant. I want speedy progress so we can put the force back in a good light. D.I. Longbottom is close to retirement. I am going to put him on extended garden leave.'

Ken and Jenny looked at each other. The conversation was coming over on the car's speaker system, so she had heard what was said. Who would take over? Would they still be on the team?

The Chief Constable's voice crackled back to life. 'So I've got to ask you. sergeant. If I were to put you in sole charge, could you make progress quickly? Do you feel you could handle it?'

Ken's surprise was clear on his face. Jenny beamed at him. She was certain that the team would be far more effective with Ken in charge. She nodded her head furiously to encourage him to agree. 'It's unexpected, sir, but I'd be grateful for the opportunity. I wouldn't let you down sir!'

'Glad to hear it! Well, that's settled then. I'll move you up to a temporary rank of detective inspector and I'll get a message to Longbottom immediately to alert him to the change.'

Ken thought quickly. 'Thank you, sir. I wonder, sir, if you have thought about a second in charge? Someone to take over my position? If not, I can recommend Jenny Watson. She's a valuable and trusted member of the team and I am sure she'll fill the role well?'

'Yes, yes. Move her up to temporary sergeant rank and get to work Jones! I'm expecting good things from you!'

'Thank you, sir. We're escorting the victim's wife to the mortuary as I speak to confirm identification of the body. As soon as that's done, I'll call the team together and get them to work!'

A bereavement counsellor was waiting at the mortuary, and she took Elyse home after the body had been confirmed as that of her husband. Ken and Jenny went back to the office and began to plan the next stage of the investigation. Ken – now D.I. Jones –

reconfigured the white board with photographs of Elyse, Alec, the body as it was originally found and a large-scale map of the area with the site of the body clearly marked. Then, late in the spring afternoon, with a mellow, rose-pink sun casting long shadows over the lawns and trees outside, he called a meeting of the new team. Only seven strong now, he knew he would have to make efficient use of everyone.

'Okay everyone, listen up. First, just to confirm that I've been put in charge of the operation from now on and Jenny has been promoted to second in command.' There were murmurs of approval and congratulation. Applause started, but Ken silenced it immediately. 'This is no reflection on our boss, Cyril, but he's been lucky enough, with his retirement so close, to be put on leave for a while. I am sure he will return to full duties soon.' No-one else hoped for that.

'Gladys – you were with Cyril when Elyse was brought in. You've been able to confirm her alibi?'

Gladys straightened. 'Yes, sarge – er boss. The other members of staff at the agency remember her there at eight thirty that morning and CCTV confirmed it.'

'Thanks, Gladys. The shot was fired in the wood at Bishop Farthing at eight at the earliest. Elyse couldn't possibly have shot him and reached Yeovil for eight thirty, even if she had a gun and was an excellent shot. Jenny – any evidence at all that she either had a gun or had any experience with one?'

'No boss. The search of her house revealed nothing and I've contacted all the local gun clubs and drawn a blank.'

'Thanks Jenny. So it's looking increasingly unlikely that Elyse was the shooter. Cyril thought it possible that she had hired someone else to do the dirty, but we haven't yet found any evidence that she would gain any significant benefit from his death and if I'm any judge of character she's totally devastated by what's happened. Geoff – what have we got from bank and insurance details?'

Geoff's lined face creased into a smile. He had a phone in one hand and the other snapped his computer into action. 'It's rather the other way round, boss. There was a policy to cover the mortgage on Mr. Bartle and that's it. His wife, however, had cover of near quarter of a million. He had a couple of thousand in his current account and savings of around twenty thousand in ISAs. If anything, he ought to have killed her!'

Ken smiled. 'So it looks more and more as if we are looking elsewhere for the killer. How about his laptop?'

Geoff lifted it so that the team had a good view of it. 'We've just managed to bypass the password and I'm trawling through the hard drive now.'

'Great work, Geoff. I want you to concentrate on that and let me know immediately if there's anything suspicious – anything that hints at a motive for murder. What was his job?'

'He was an accountant, boss.'

'Uhm. There maybe something there. Could be he found out something about a client's business dealings that was sensitive enough for him to be killed. Check through emails – everything. Pick out anything that looks even slightly out of the ordinary.'

'Got it, boss!'

There was a pause and Ken stood tall as he waited to ensure that he had everyone's full attention. 'The body was officially identified this afternoon. Tomorrow morning, we release the name to the press and give a briefing. I want to request help from the public. Anyone with any information will be asked to contact our helpline. I'm asking Nick and Gina to man the phones here and take these calls. As we know, a high proportion of them will be irrelevant to the case – especially in Bishop Farthing (Ken and Jenny exchanged smiles, remembering their experience of interviewing some of its eccentric inhabitants) – but everything must be recorded and cross referenced.

'Because Cyril thought the case was tied up, I don't recall him meeting the couple who found the body. Jenny and I will call on them first thing tomorrow. Jenny – you have the number. Can you fix that up for nine tomorrow?' She nodded, pleased to be the one he chose and happily conscious of being his second in command. 'Okay, it's getting late. Let's all get an early night. A fresh start in the morning and let's get this tied up!'

There was a general buzz of appreciation.

They recognised that their new boss had a sensible plan and was being considerate of their work life balance. Two innovations that were both welcome. Only Jenny looked slightly sad. She knew where Ken was going that evening. Every time she thought of the young, attractive pathologist she felt plain and dumpy.

13

Ken cradled the glass of Beaujolais in his hand as he gazed out of the wide window of the high-rise block at the sea and the Bournemouth coastline. The sun was setting, touching everything with gold.

He was in the difficult position of someone at the start of a relationship. Unsure whether or not he was to stay the night, he didn't know if this should be his only alcoholic drink of the evening. Sheila walked in with a steaming bowl of pasta and placed it on the table along with a large fork and serving spoon.

'You have an amazing view from here. I'm jealous!'

'I was lucky. I got a first-home buyer deal and had a timely legacy from my grandfather. It was still too expensive. You pay an arm and a leg for the view. Much more sensible to buy on the other side of the block. Great views of the car park from there! We'll go out on the balcony later. The smell of the sea air is quite something! Sit yourself down!'

He had not had time to change. He was still wearing the shirt and jeans he'd had on all day. As he watched her working in the kitchen area. he suddenly felt underdressed and at a disadvantage. She had stripped off the work clothes he'd last seen her in and had a shower. She looked fresh and radiant. The dress she wore, a lovely turquoise blue, clung to her and emphasised the curves of her body. Probably not silk, he thought, but it could have been. It flared over her hips and fell gracefully almost to her knees. It swayed with her as she moved. He couldn't take his eyes off it for a long minute.

Ken took his seat and Sheila swirled into the kitchen, reappearing with a bowl of meat sauce in one hand and a plate of garlic bread in the other. Ken topped up her glass, but left his own half full. He waited for her to comment. If she said, 'Aren't you having more?' it would point to an invitation to stay the night. If she didn't, well…

Maybe she hadn't noticed. Sheila forked a confusion of spaghetti onto his plate and then hers. She pushed the bowl of Bolognaise sauce towards him and offered him a serving ladle. Ken spooned on a reasonable portion, less than half, not wanting to seem pushy or greedy. Sheila helped herself to a slightly smaller amount. Watching her weight?

'How long have you lived here?'

'Just under a year. Still getting it sorted!' It looked very sorted, Ken thought. It was much better furnished than his two-bedroom terrace starter home and he'd been there nearly four. The two sofas were off-white soft leather. Very stylish as well as comfortable. The prints on the wall were classy – abstract and tasteful. Ken wasn't sure who the artist was. Miro? Kandinsky? He didn't want to ask in case he made a fool of himself. He concentrated instead on the spaghetti, winding it round his fork. She laughed as a string of it escaped from his mouth, but it seemed good humoured. He laughed in return.

'There's no polite way to eat spaghetti!' she joked and made a similar mess of her own. Ken relaxed.

'It's delicious! You're an excellent cook!'

'Mainly from packets!' She used a slice of garlic bread to wipe some of the sauce from the side of her plate and chewed it.

'The chief phoned me today. He's put the D. I. on garden leave till his retirement's due. He asked me to take over. I've been given a temporary promotion to inspector level.'

'The wisest thing he's ever done! Congratulations!'

'It's not permanent.'

'It will be. You've got what it takes. Everyone knows it.' She raised her glass. 'Here's to you! Detective Inspector Jones!'

'Thank you! Cheers!' He took a sip from his glass. The level was getting low. He waited for her to notice. If she suggested he fill his glass, it would give him a chance to say that he couldn't, that he had to think about the drive home. Then she could say, no stay the night. He waited. She continued to eat.

'It's an interesting case. I am sure that the wife had nothing to do with the killing. But so far, we haven't found anyone with a motive. We're going public tomorrow with the victim's name to see if we can get any further leads.'

'Sounds like a plan.' She put down her fork and looked him in the eyes. Hers were hazel brown, he noticed, With dark lashes. He felt a stirring of feelings for her. 'Let's not talk shop. Save that for tomorrow.' The look she was giving him, along with the teasing smile, was, he was sure, causing him to blush. She was turning him on. Did she notice? Was she feeling the same? She spoke slowly now as if this was the start of a very important conversation for them both. 'Let's talk about us.'

'I'd love to.'

'I like you, Ken. I like you very much.'

'I feel the same. I liked you the first time I saw you.'

Sheila looked at him carefully. Was he a smooth talker? Or genuine? 'But it's complicated. There's something I've got to tell you.'

'You're already married. You've got six children, three of them black!'

They laughed together. Sheila waved a hand to silence him. 'Don't be silly. No, I'm not married. And I'd have had to start at fourteen to have six children!'

164

'Two sets of triplets?'

'This is serious. Listen. I'm not married but there is somebody else. I'm already in a relationship.'

'I guessed you were.' Ken wasn't sure of his feelings. Was she going to tell him that there was no hope for him? Or was she just sharing a problem that she wanted him to help her sort out, so that they could be together?

'I want to end it. I want a new start. And that could be with you - if you're willing.'

'Just try me!'

'But it's complicated. It's with – I wasn't going to tell you this, but I think I must – you must promise to keep this absolutely to yourself!' Ken nodded, feeling nervous. This sounded mysterious and worrying. 'It's with my boss.'

There was a long moment of silence. Ken tried to take this in. It was hard for him to reconcile this. 'Your boss? You mean Harold?'

She nodded. Ken tried to be tactful, but it was not in his interests to be in any way supportive of this arrangement. 'But – he must be a lot older than you?'

Sheila nodded. 'At first it didn't seem a problem – I didn't even think about it. But now I do, more and more. He's in his fifties. A different generation. And his tastes and interests don't coincide with mine. It's becoming clearer and clearer that it won't work in the long run. And – this is important – he can't give me children.'

Ken gasped. 'Can I say – something rather forward?'

'Go on.'

'I would want to have children. With you.'

Sheila smiled. 'I'm rather pleased to hear it.'

'So why don't you dump him? Tell him you've realised it won't work? That it's time to move on…'

'I will. But like I said, it's complicated. He's a nice man. He's been truly kind and helpful to me. I have to do this in my own time, in my own way.' Ken didn't like the sound of this. And it didn't sound a good plan. Selfishly, he wanted her to free herself as soon as possible so that he could be with her. Could sleep with her.

166

'How long? How long would it take you to finish with him?'

'I don't know. It may be soon. It depends how he responds.'

'He'll never give you up!'

'That's a sort of compliment. I think. Thank you. He'll have to. But think of it as a kind of test. If you think I'm worth waiting for, if you'll give me the space to do this in my own way, it'll be a big plus for you. Can you wait?'

Ken chewed on his lip. This was unexpected. And it went against his manhood to stand in line behind a balding man in his fifties who couldn't have kids. 'While I'm waiting…while you extricate yourself from this…will you be having sex with him?'

Sheila's eyebrows raised slightly at this. 'That's very personal.' She paused, then, 'I might. It depends. It's none of your business. You must let me do this as I think best.'

'This is hard.'

'Yes,' she agreed. And then, with genuine sympathy in her voice, 'I know it's hard. I know I'm asking a lot.'

'It sounds like a test.'

'Maybe it is. Partly. But it's what I need to do. He's my boss, remember. Just be patient, Ken. Just for a little while. That's not too much to ask, is it?'

'Maybe not.' But Ken was far from convinced.

Sheila raised her glass. 'To the future!'

'Our future.'

'Together! Now it's getting late. I've got to ask you to go. But first...' Sheila walked round the table and sat on his knee. She kissed him full on the lips. A long, very sexy kiss. 'Just a little on account!'

It was a very thoughtful Ken who left the apartment block. He wasn't sure if this was going to work or how long he could put up with knowing that the woman he loved was with another man. It was late, but he didn't want to go straight home. He was angry and frustrated. Ken tried to avoid 'self-abuse' as the RE teacher at school had called it, warning the boys that it was sinful and bad for their health. His advice on sexual morality had lost some of its force with his pupils when he was discovered in an adulterous relationship with the art mistress.

Ken set off back to headquarters where there was a small gym in the basement. Once there he worked out on the weights and then thrashed his body on a treadmill before a refreshing cold shower. Ken believed keeping fit and strong was essential to his role, as well as important for his general health. It was two in the morning before he sank into his lonely bed and fell into a deep but troubled sleep.

14

By eight the next morning, Ken and Jenny were in his car, negotiating the narrow lanes that lead to Bishop Farthing. Jenny was quiet. She had taken extra care with her hair and make-up that morning, for no special reason. Well, she was travelling with her new boss and wanted to feel confident about herself. She took a sideways glance at Ken. He hadn't shaved. It looked good – sort of swarthy and masculine – but it was unusual for him. She wondered why. Had he been up so late with Sheila that he'd been in too much of a rush this morning to get ready properly? He hadn't stayed the night – he wasn't wearing the same shirt. She remembered everything about him. She knew it had been a plain blue Oxford yesterday. Today, he wore a navy suit and a white shirt with a dark blue pinstripe she'd often admired before. So he had been home. He seemed preoccupied. Maybe the evening hadn't gone well. If so, Jenny wasn't triumphant. She was caring enough to be concerned for his feelings.

He stopped the car in one of the few passing places and consulted the satnav again. He silently cursed Dorset villages that are so rambling – where houses don't have numbers, only names, some of which are hard to spot, and even some stretches of road are anonymous. Bishop Farthing is a village with no clear identity. Apart from a shop, a church and a village hall (where the gardening club meet and creaky old ladies assemble one night a week to do a form of rhythmic exercise to music that has to be seen to be believed) there is no centre to the community. The inhabitants are friendly, neighbourly, but so scattered they don't all know or recognise each other. The result of this is that friendliness can easily turn to suspicion if something untoward happens and this leads to fearful messages on the local website. As a result, Dorset folk who live in rival villages, such as Bishop's Caundle and Piddlehinton now refer to our village as Bishop Farting.

Ken pinpointed the approximate position of Beth's house and parked outside Mrs Simpkins' – to her great excitement. She directed them to the house opposite, whilst fluttering her eyelashes at the detective and doing her best impression of a pretty, young girl – much to Jenny's amusement.

Beth welcomed them into her home. Always the detective, Ken looked round the lounge for clues about her interests and taste. Beth herself was about five feet four, pretty and slender. She wore no make-up and was, he guessed, approaching fifty. The room was decorated in a chic, country-cottage style, with Laura Ashley fabrics and comfortable sofas. He saw no sign of a male presence, although he understood that she had a partner.

'Peter couldn't make it this early,' Beth apologised. 'He has two tutorials this morning. If you need to speak with him, he can arrange it for this afternoon.'

'He doesn't live here then? Is he far away?'

'No – about three hundred yards down Orchard Lane. We have separate homes.'

'But you went walking together the day before yesterday?'

'Yes. We do most things together,' Beth smiled. 'But this arrangement suits us best. We both have our space.'

Ken nodded. 'It makes a lot of sense. I think many marriages would last longer if people had more time apart!'

Jenny tutted. 'That's very cynical!'

'Cynical and realistic,' Ken agreed. 'Well anyway, let's see what Beth can tell us and then we'll decide whether or not we need to interview Peter as well. Beth – can I have your full name?'

'Bethesda Monks – Mrs.'

As Jenny took notes, Ken looked up in surprise. 'Your parents were very religious?'

'No – far from it. They were hippies. They named me after the place where I was…conceived!'

Ken looked embarrassed. Jenny was amused. He continued, 'So you went for a morning walk – do you remember the exact time you reached the wood?'

'Yes, because it was special. We don't walk every morning, but we'd heard the bluebells were full out and so we made the effort. It's quite a sight.'

Jenny had her pen poised over her open pad. 'They're beautiful. We've seen them. But the time?'

'Oh sorry. We left here at eight. So it would have been no later than half past by the time we reached the wood.'

Ken leaned forward. 'Think hard, Beth. Apart from finding the body, was there anything else unusual? Anything you noticed?' Beth looked confused. 'Did you hear a gunshot, for example?'

'There were two sort of cracking noises!' Suddenly Beth was more animated as the memories came flooding back. 'Not loud bangs. More like twigs snapping – but they sounded far off…'

'Were you in the wood then?'

'No – walking down the lane. We were some way from the woods so I never put it together!'

'That's okay – so that would have been when? About quarter past?'

'Yes – more or less.'

'That's really helpful Beth. I think you heard the gunshots, and this gives us the exact time of the shooting!'

'He was shot?' Beth started in alarm.

'Yes. We'll be going public with the details later this morning and now we can give an actual time.' Ken was relieved. The more details he could give in the briefing, the more knowledgeable the police would seem and pinpointing the time of the shooting might stir memories in others. 'And when you reached the murder scene, the body was lying face down?'

'Yes. At first we thought he was resting – or praying – Muslims pray like that, don't they?'

'It wasn't a Muslim. It was Elyse's husband, Alec Bartle. Do you know him?'

'Oh – I know them both! How terrible for her!'

'Can you think of any reason why anyone would target Alec?'

'No – I only know them socially. They were so nice! Why would anyone?'

'We need to understand why he was in the wood. Have you ever seen him there before – in the early morning?'

'No. We only walk there occasionally and not always so early. But sometimes – maybe twice this last week – I've noticed him, now you mention it…'

'Noticed him?'

'Walking past. He'd have to walk past this house to reach the wood. I have seen him, walk past, quite early – but I never thought much about it. But now you mention it, he must have been going there…'

Ken was satisfied. A pattern was beginning to emerge, though he couldn't be sure yet what it meant. 'This is really helpful, Beth. You're a star! We'll be checking any CCTV footage from house cameras – though I am not sure there will be any round here,' Beth shook her head, 'and windscreen footage. We may be able to pin down his movements over the last few days.' He checked with Jenny that her notes were keeping up and was impressed, as always, with her efficiency. 'Is there anything else? Anything at all you remember?'

Beth looked first at Jenny. And then at Ken. 'Well, yes. There was the woman.'

Elyse's sister had stayed the night and was clearing the breakfast things. She had worked hard at trying to get Elyse to eat and had finally succeeded in getting some toast down her. Elyse hadn't realised how much she needed company and was deeply grateful for Angela's presence. Her sister was a PE teacher and so was determined not to allow Elyse to mope. She had organised a list of actions that needed to be carried out. They were not ones that Elyse would have chosen. Later that day they had to visit the undertaker. Mr. Jones would have called at the house, but Angela wanted to get Elyse out. She was wearing a smart Nike tracksuit as she called to Elyse from the kitchen. 'Get ready girl! We've to see the bank manager in thirty minutes!' Elyse half expected her to blow a whistle. But the home did not seem quite so empty and echoey now that Angela had moved in.

She ran a brush through her hair. She had

made an effort to dress smartly, but she couldn't wear the smart grey business suit that she had on when she was arrested. It had too many terrible memories. She wore a sober, dark grey dress that she had sometimes worn for the office. Her boss didn't like his female staff to dress too prettily. There had been too many instances of male clients making overtures to them. When looking over properties, some had concentrated too much on looking over the lady who was showing them round...

Last night Elyse and Angela had argued over Alec's things. Angela was for getting rid of them – shipping them to the nearest charity shop. She had laughed when she saw that Elyse had put his last discarded clothes through the washing machine, ironed the shirts, folded them neatly and placed them neatly in his wardrobe. But Elyse wasn't ready to part with them yet, even though she had no idea what to do with his clothes, his golf clubs, the models he had built (he insisted they were models, she saw them as toys). She was aching and lonely. Parting with all Alec's belongings was heart breaking. It was a finality that she wasn't yet ready to face.

She thought bitterly of the crime stories and

films she had seen. The widow was simply a plot necessity. Once she had identified the body, she was forgotten, lost to the plot. Reality was so very different. Angela was sympathetic but sensible. There was no point in clinging to things that could only bring sad memories. A clean sheet was what was wanted. A fresh start. But Elyse was not yet ready for that.

15

Beth was leading Ken and Jenny into the bluebell wood, following the exact path that she had taken with Peter on that fateful morning. When they reached the place where they had found Alec's body, she paused and scanned the perimeter. Then she pointed to the gap in the fence that Annette had noticed. 'She was over there!'

Ken squinted towards the hedge line. It was late in the morning and the sun had moved round so that it was in his eyes, 'Was she in the wood?'

'No, the other side of the fence. In the field.'

They walked with difficulty through the undergrowth and reached the fence. 'Can you describe her?'

'We only caught a glimpse, and she was quite far away.' Ken knew that this was true. Beth would have had to peer through the trees and bushes to catch sight of her and she was at least a hundred yards from them.

Jenny tried to help by offering basic suggestions. 'Was she young – old?'

'Young I would say. She moved swiftly. Perhaps in her twenties?'

This was something. Jenny tried again as Ken pushed through the break in the fence and scanned the terrain beyond. 'What was she wearing? A dress? Slacks?'

Beth's forehead creased in concentration. 'It was a dress. It was short. And dark tights – black. And the dress was black too. As soon as she saw us, she started to run, as if she was afraid of us…The short dress meant she could move quickly.'

By this time, they were all through the fence and standing on the edge of the open field. To their surprise, two deer broke cover only a few yards away and sprinted away towards a distant tree line. Beth waved her hand across the scene. 'They'll be from the deer park. This all belongs to the manor house.'

Jenny remembered Annette's account of her

dream. Probably irrelevant, but it was an odd coincidence — if that's what it was. 'Did she make any sound? Did she scream, for instance?'

Beth looked confused. 'Scream? No – I don't think so. It all happened so fast. I think she said something, but I couldn't make out what it was. I don't think it was English…'

'Was she running towards the manor house?' They could see just a glimpse of it on the horizon. 'Could she belong there?'

Beth shrugged. 'I don't know. We keep away. Most of the women round here know to keep their distance.' She remembered her encounter with his lordship, when he had tricked her to go behind a marquee with him at a village fete and had groped her, lecherously, before she managed to break away from him.

Jenny was quick on the uptake. She had experience of men as well. 'He's a bit too handy. Is he?' Beth nodded and they exchanged a knowing smile.

Ken was thoughtful. 'We need to track this woman down. At the very least, she could be a useful witness. Our first stop should be at the manor!'

Beth sighed. 'Good luck there!'

They walked Beth back to her home and then rang the office to get a postcode for the manor house. It was Geoff he responded. 'Funny you should ask that, boss. I was just going to call you. There's something suspicious in the emails on the victim's computer.'

'Just a second. I'll put this on loudspeaker so that Jen can hear too.'

'Right. Boss.'

'There's something that ties Alec Bartle to the manor?'

'Right. He was the accountant handling the estate's finances. There are several messages between them over the last few weeks. It looks as if he had found a problem – a discrepancy – in the accounts. The estate included a number of commercial properties and some residential ones. Three of these are in Southampton, near the docks. They're big places. Apparently set up for multiple occupation. They'd all been set up as student rooms until last year when all three were let to the same man. And he was negotiating for a fourth.'

Ken nodded. This was odd. 'Any idea what

he wanted them for?'

'No. But Alec was questioning it. The emails are asking for more details about the arrangement. He may have suspected money laundering and if this was true, as the accountant, he could be liable.'

'Any idea what was making him suspect something fishy?'

'Yes boss. It's the money involved! As student rooms, these houses were bringing in a steady five hundred a week. Once the new owner took over, the income from them doubled. A thousand a week from each property – and only five bedrooms in each!'

Ken nodded. 'Only two ways of getting that sort of money. The man renting them is selling drugs or vice. And I can't think why you'd need five bedroomed houses for drugs!'

'That's what I thought boss. Shall I get in touch with the Hampshire vice team?'

'Hold back a while, Geoff. Let's see what we find out at the manor!'

Right, boss!'

'One more thing. You think he was

concerned about money laundering at the mansion. Was he involved in anything fishy himself? Anything that would have tied him with organised crime?'

'No boss. Unless there are bank accounts we haven't found yet. But there are three transactions that stick out as odd. He sent small amounts of money abroad. Through a company that changes sterling into foreign currencies. I could get in touch and see where they went to.'

'Thanks, Geoff. Do that,'

'Okay boss. But these were trifling amounts. Forty or fifty pounds each time.'

'Still worth following up.'

Ken weaved the car through the narrow twisting lanes that led from Bishop Farthing to the manor. It is said that Stephen Squinteye, the Saxon road planner designated by King Alfred as the person to determine the road system for England, was not a well organised person. Apparently, the day that he spread open the map of Dorset and began to mark out the lanes and byways he had arrived at work with a pair of compasses but no ruler. If this is true, it explains a great deal. And as Ken twisted and swerved round the endless hairpins and blind bends, he would have liked very much to have encountered the same Stephen and told him what he thought of his work.

He pulled up at the gates that led, via a long, gravelled drive, to the manor's impressive columned entrance. They could not proceed any further. The gates were locked. Ken opened the car door and pressed a button on a rather ancient intercom that was attached with rusting screws to one of the gate posts. No answer. He pressed again several times, with greater force, in the hope that this would make the system ring louder in the hall. After several minutes, he finally got a response. The voice seemed to be that of an elderly retainer with an accent that dripped with old school contempt for members of the public.

'I am sorry to tell you that you have wasted your journey. The house is not open to the general public.'

Ken bridled as he registered the arrogance of this, spoken in an upper-class, public-school accent. His response was heavy with sarcasm. 'Actually, my man, we are not here as a tour party. We are police officers. We are here to question a young woman who we believe is a resident at the hall. We believe she can help us with our enquiries into a serious crime.'

This would have been a sufficient put down to make most men fall into line, but the tone of the voice on the intercom suggested that the speaker was unimpressed. 'Indeed. Since the sad and untimely death of her ladyship, there have been few female persons in residence at the manor. One is the cook, a substantial lady in her early or late fifties, and a domestic maid who is, I believe, of younger years.'

By this time, Jenny had joined Ken by the intercom and she raised her eyebrows at this, wondering how her boss would cope. He was brusque. 'It sounds as if the maid is the one we need to interview, but to be safe, we'll talk to both.'

'Certainly, sir. Unfortunately, his lordship is absent today. He is at Westminster. There is an important debate on the budget, I understand.'

'That's fine. We don't need to speak to his lordship at this time.'

'And he has given me strict instructions to admit no visitors in his absence.'

Ken was beginning to lose patience. 'We're not visitors. We are police officers going about our lawful business.'

'That may well be, sir. And when his lordship returns, I shall certainly inform him of your desire to interview members of his staff.'

'That won't do. We are investigating a serious crime and if you refuse us entry, I have to inform you that you may be guilty of obstructing a police enquiry. I must insist that you allow us entry!'

'I see, sir.' The disembodied voice dropped a couple of notes and the honeyed tone became more steely. 'In that case, you will have brought a warrant?'

Ken moved away in disgust, refusing to give the man the courtesy of a reply. Jenny's eyes were questioning. 'Is he just following instructions? Or is he hiding something?'

Before Ken could respond, his phone rang. It was Nick back at base. 'Hi boss. I've done a search of gun licences in the Bishop Farthing area. I'm checking for shotguns. I know the shooter may not be local, but I thought we should check them anyway.'

'Good work, Nige. What have you found?'

'Only three altogether, boss. One of them is where you are now – the manor. They've got a whole armoury! I assume it's for bird shoots.'

'Interesting. Can you call at the other two houses and bring the guns in so we can check them against the shell cases we've found at the scene?'

'Right boss. I'll leave the manor to you then.'

'It's not going to be that simple. Can you apply to a magistrate – do it straight away – and get a warrant to allow us to search the property? They're not allowing us in!'

'Bloody hell! I'll get onto it straight away, boss!'

Ken and Jenny stared at each other with a look of amused helplessness. Then Ken shrugged and declared, 'There's nothing we can do until the warrant comes through. Lunch?'

Jenny smiled and nodded. A quiet lunch with Ken seemed a delightful prospect, even though she knew she wasn't in the running.

16

The Greyhound was almost empty and they had no trouble finding a corner table where they wouldn't be overheard. If they were to discuss any detail of the case, it would not do to broadcast it. They both ordered a Ploughman's and two soft drinks. Television cops are hard drinkers but in today's modern force, alcohol is frowned on when on duty and, now that Ken had been promoted, he was determined to set a good example.

Jenny looked thoughtful. 'I know it's odd, boss – but some things seem to be fitting together. This young woman that Annette alerted us too – she thought she was screaming – and then Beth and Peter saw a woman matching that description running away after the killing. We go to interview her and we're not allowed in the house. It looks fishy.'

'But what's the connection with the victim?'

Jenny chewed for a moment on a small lump of cheddar. 'Well, we still don't know why he had started walking down to the woods in the early morning. Beth said she'd seen him a few times in the last couple of weeks. It's quite a distance from where he lived. Why would he do it? His wife knew nothing about it. Had he suddenly become a committed nature lover – or…'

'Or he was meeting someone there. Is Elyse telling the truth? Did she suspect something? It would be the nearest we've come so far to a motive. But it's a bit drastic to take a shotgun to the woods, find him at it, and shoot him. It's the stuff of Italian opera rather than Dorset soap!'

'And we know she couldn't have done it anyway.' Jenny dipped a square of cheese into a blob of Branston Pickle. 'She hasn't got a gun. She has a solid alibi. And she's heartbroken.'

Ken nodded. 'So we've got a possible motive, but no suspect!' He took a long sip of his shandy. 'No worry. It's only the third day. We're still waiting for a complete download of Alec's computer. If there was anything suspicious in his life – in his business dealings or his personal life, we should get it from there.

Laptops and mobiles have become our best informants!'

Jenny felt unusually brave. The intimacy of the place, along with the closeness between them – even though it was only a professional one – gave her the confidence to ask, 'And speaking of personal – how are things between you and your gorgeous lady friend?' She smiled as if to imply that it was just a friendly enquiry and of no particular interest to her. 'Are we talking relationship yet?'

Ken shook his head. It was actually a good chance to talk about Sheila. He needed to sort out his feelings and he thought of Jenny as a neutral and dispassionate listener. 'It's complicated.' He smiled. He could hardly believe what he was telling her. 'She having an affair with her boss.'

Jenny's eyebrows shot up. 'You're joking me!' Ken shook his head, resignedly. 'Harry Mekson?'

Ken nodded, showing no emotion.

'Doctor Mekson! He's old enough to be her dad! He's past it, surely!'

Ken's look hardened. 'Clearly not.'

Jenny shivered as she imagined an elderly man, with his wrinkled and balding head, making out on her. 'And she really prefers him to you?' Admiring Ken as she did, this was beyond her comprehension.

Ken shook his head with an attempt at modesty. 'I don't think so. I really don't. But she wants me to hold back until she sorts it out.'

Jenny was shocked. 'So you're supposed to hang around while she still sees him? She's got a nerve!'

Ken secretly agreed. He sighed, 'It is what it is. We'll see how it works out. I'm not waiting for ever.'

Jenny nodded her head vigorously. She agreed without a trace of self-interest. 'Bloody right! There's plenty more fish in the sea! You shouldn't be expected to put up with it!'

Ken was feeling moody and bitter as he excused himself and visited the gents. Jenny said she'd wait for him outside. When he stepped out into the sunshine, he was blinded momentarily. When his eyes adjusted to the bright light, he made out Jenny over by the car. Two yobs were standing close to her, leering at her legs. For the first time he noticed that she was wearing a pretty dress, in a deep plum pink fabric, slightly short, the hem just above her knees. One advantage of working for CID, they could wear civilian dress. Ken had no problem with women dressing attractively. He was not one of those on the force who thought women were asking for trouble if they walked around looking sexy. It was up to them what they chose to wear, and there was no excuse for men who molest them.

Looking at Jenny dispassionately for the first time that day, Ken realised that she was attractive, and these two youths clearly agreed. One of them moved up to her, more aggressively than Ken liked. He was too far away to hear what they were saying but recognised that Jenny was becoming distressed. The closest yob began to grope her. She pushed him away. The other joined in and they started to push her towards the back of the building. Ken moved in. He hoped a not-so-friendly warning would be enough to revise their thinking on the subject of male/female relationships. One of his pet hates was violence of men against women – the bullying, the feeble attempt to prove your masculinity by forcing yourself on a woman.

The two youths turned as Ken approached. They were both about five ten, with a tragically high opinion of their ability to deal out punishment. Ken was deceptively calm. 'I think it would be best if you moved away from that lady.'

'Yeah?' The one who'd accosted Jenny stood firm, his legs braced slightly apart, an arrogant smile on his face. Ken's accent convinced them that he wasn't hard, just a middle-class meddler. 'What's it to you mate?'

His friend was equally cocky. 'Yeah – you shagging her or what?'

Ken took no notice. He continued to walk calmly and steadily towards the two. He was prepared to give them due warning. He reached into his jacket to produce his police identity card. But before he could complete the movement, the first yob reacted, assuming he was reaching for a weapon. He pulled a knife from his jacket. 'Bloody watch it, mate! Less you want a bleeding blade up your gut!'

Ken had had enough. The time for being reasonable was over. These two were guilty of sexual assault and now threatening a police officer with a knife. He weighed up the likely moves of the two youths. The one with the knife was sporting a dark facial stubble. No doubt he thought it made him look tough. In truth, it made him look unwashed. Ken knew from watching him for only a few seconds that he was untrained and clumsy. He could take him easily.

The yob telegraphed his first move. He lunged forward with the knife pointing at Ken's chest. The detective slipped to one side, used his left hand to catch the wrist of the hand holding the weapon and pulled him off balance. Before his antagonist had time to realise the danger he was in, Ken crashed his right fist into his startled face. It connected fully with the nose, which exploded from the force of the blow, sending blood and phlegm spattering over the boy's eyes, lips and stubble. In a red rage, the youth twisted round to face his opponent and tried to aim a kick at him, even though he was almost blind. His eyes stung and wept from the salt of the blood that had smothered them. Ken aimed a punch at his solar plexus. It thudded home, burying itself in the chest. His would-be assassin collapsed to the ground like a bag of cement, struggling to breathe.

His companion would have been wise to flee when he saw the fate of his friend. Instead, in an unwise display of loyalty, he too pulled out a knife. More cautious after seeing how the stranger had dispatched his friend, he began to circle Ken watching for the chance to strike. Ken held back. He was confident that he could deal with the scumbag, but knew it would be best to let him make the first move. The youth made a critical error. His circling movement left him a couple of feet in front of Jenny, with his back to her. He didn't even think about her. She was a mere woman. No threat to him. He would stab her meddling friend and then deal with his bint. Ken's face was expressionless as Jenny winked at him and then attacked from the rear, one arm around the yob's neck, the other firmly fixed on the wrist of the arm that held the knife.

The youth was so stunned with surprise that, for a second, he failed to react, pulled off balance with his mouth hanging open. Ken gestured to Jenny to push him forward. He was so tempted to send his foot hard and true into the idiot's testicles. It could have been the end of his interest in sex, but it could cause serious damage and that would involve Ken in weeks of paperwork and trouble with IPCC. As she pushed him towards Ken, her boss closed the yob's mouth with an uppercut that would have felled a heavy weight boxer. He crumpled to the ground like a rag doll, unconscious.

His companion was just beginning to reclaim the power of speech. He glanced sideways, fearfully, at Ken. 'Bloody hell, mate. No bloody need for that. We was just messing about!'

'So was I!' responded Ken, drily. 'Lucky for you I wasn't serious. Or you'd be in intensive care.'

Jenny walked briskly to their car - apparently a standard powerful saloon, its blue lights concealed in the front grill - and brought back two pairs of handcuffs. Ken rang in for a van to take the yobs into custody, charged with assault and possession of a dangerous weapon, just for starters. Ken went to check the pub's CCTV images to check that the incident had been fully recorded, as the louts sat, forlornly, back-to-back, reconsidering their attitudes to young women and the carrying of knives.

It was then that Ken's phone rang. It was the Chief Constable. 'Afternoon, Jones!'

'Sir!'

'Just checking in with you. I've had a report that you're requesting a warrant to enter the manor house just outside Bishop Farthing…'

'Correct, sir.'

'And this is absolutely necessary, is it? You see I had an agreement with Longbottom that the manor would be kept out of any investigation. His lordship is getting on in years. National figure. War hero. We need to be, well, extremely sensitive. If the press get hold of it, there could be very bad publicity. For us and him. I need hardly remind you of past searches of the homes of the famous that have come back to bite us!'

'I understand, sir. But there's a woman who seems to be in residence at the manor who was seen leaving the crime scene just after the shooting. We really need to speak to her. And when we called at the manor, we were refused entry. There's also a link between the victim and the business dealings of the estate.'

'Understood. Look, I can see that you need to obtain entry, old chap – but I'd rather keep it low key. A warrant could bring the reporters round – if only because someone at head office could leak the information. Sad, but true. Leave it to me, son. I'll contact the manor and tell them to let you in. I'm sure they'll be reasonable if the request comes from me. Just go ahead and assume you'll now gain entry. If I hit any snags, I'll let the warrant request go ahead. But I think the mention of it will bring them round.'

'Thank you, sir. We've two yobs to deal with for sexual assault. As soon as they're picked up. We'll go back to the manor.'

'That'll give me time to get them to see reason. Go ahead, Jones – but be, well, discreet.'

'Understood sir.'

Ken was inwardly fuming. This had reminded him again of the strength of the old boy network. His own father, who had never risen above the rank of sergeant because of his refusal to join their clique, had been frustrated in a gay murder enquiry by the protection that the rich and famous could expect from their friends in high places. He'd go along with the Chief just so long as it didn't compromise the operation. But no further.

17

Half an hour later, Ken and Jenny were driving again along the half mile drive that led to the manor. It was, it seemed, the only decent stretch of straight road in Dorset. It was lined on each side with ancient beech trees that stood sentinel, guarding the approach. They drove through their dappled shade up to the forbidding gates.

Ken remained in his seat, staring at the closed entrance. He wondered whether he'd given the Chief enough time to clear the way for them. Maybe wait another couple of minutes before facing up to the unfriendly voice at the other end of the line. Jenny laid her hand on his. 'Thank you.'

'Thank you? For what?'

Jenny smiled sweetly. 'For helping me out back there!'

'I reckon you could have probably dealt with them without me!'

'No. There were two of them. You were my knight in shining armour!'

Ken paused and considered the way things had turned out, 'I was probably too hard on them. But if there's one thing I hate it's little men who try to look big by throwing their weight around. Especially if they use force against women because they're too cowardly to take on a man. They're scum and a disgrace to decent men everywhere.'

Jenny leaned towards him and shyly, in a move that took him very much by surprise, she gave him a gentle kiss on the cheek. 'Actually boss, that's one of the sweetest things about you!' Ken's phone rang before he had a chance to come up with a suitable response to this. It was Geoff, with news of a breakthrough on the dead man's phone.

'We've had a response from the phone provider, boss, and they've helped us unlock it. We've scrolled through most of the calls, texts and photos.'

'Great work, Geoff. What's it showing us?'

'There's good news and bad, boss. The bad first. There's shit all to indicate that there was another woman. I know you're about to interview one, but there's no record of any contact between him and a bird. No romantic emojis, no sexy texts, nothing.'

'So how does this woman fit in? We've got evidence of her presence at the scene. And she's his only motive for these visits to the woods…'

'Beats me, boss. But there's something else. The victim was texting someone who works at the manor. His name is Carl and he appears to be an estate manager or in charge of the manor's business affairs. The texts aren't friendly.'

'In what way?'

'There only a few clues about what was up between them, but it looks as if Alec had discovered something suspicious in the accounts. He was asking for – well – clarification. And from what I can guess, this Carl was mighty unwilling to go along with it.'

'Thanks Geoff. I hate to ask this, but can you access all the financial information on the estate and see if there any major discrepancies that would be a cause for concern?'

'Already onto it, boss. I'll let you know as soon as I've got anything!'

'Thanks, Geoff.' He turned to Jenny. 'Okay, let's try to get in, shall we?'

Jenny was quiet, thinking through the implications of what she'd heard. It didn't make sense. It seemed clear that the woman had something to add to the enquiry, but it didn't seem that Alec had any contact with her. And what secrets would the manor hold? Ken pressed the intercom. He was met by the same cultured voice, dripping with money and public-school arrogance. 'I am sorry to inform you that the house is closed to visitors today.'

Ken was prepared for this. In a rather comical imitation of the intercom's accent, he replied. 'That is no problem at all, my good man. We aren't here for a house tour. We have the authority of the Chief Constable to commence a search of the premises!'

'Indeed, sir. I have received a communication from your superior officer requesting that I grant you entry. If you would be so kind as to wait a moment, I will operate the mechanism that causes the gates to give entrance.'

'Most kind!' Ken and Jenny exchanged amused glances. Jenny in particular was looking forward to meeting the body that went with this very annoying voice. There was a loud click and then two electric motors whirred into action, causing the metal gates to swing slowly open.

As they drove down the gravel drive and parked by the impressive front entrance, with its columned portico and its heavy oak doors, Ken gave final instructions to Jenny. 'We've been left in an awkward position. The chief has got us entry, but without a warrant, we're on difficult ground. Are we allowed to carry out a search? We certainly need to get hold of the guns and get them to forensics.

'Here's the plan. When we get in, you ask to interview the two women. Hopefully the posh talker will have to arrange it and that should leave me free to snoop around.'

'Will do, boss.'

Jenny left the car, smoothing down her dress, perhaps in an unconscious effort to look smart at the entrance to such an impressive mansion. Ken was wearing a dark blue suit and an open-necked shirt. In a subtle protest against the views on dress held by polite society, he had scorned polished black leather shoes in favour of navy-coloured trainers.

They stood at the entrance and stared at the doors, their wood stained dark with age, reinforced with blackened metal straps and hinges. They had withstood the Commonwealth forces in the English Civil War and threatened to keep out the modern forces of democracy. A long metal chain hung down beside the right-hand door. To Ken, it looked rather like an old-fashioned lavatory pull. He yanked it down firmly and from somewhere deep inside the house a bell was heard to jangle. It sounded cross, as if annoyed to be disturbed so abruptly from its slumber. A long period of silence – and then the sound of footsteps approaching from the interior, slowly and reluctantly. A bolt was pulled back and one of the doors creaked open.

It revealed a thin, lanky man in his late forties with a slightly sunken face and watery blue eyes. His skin was sallow, as if he were rarely in the sun. He greeted them with assumed deference. 'Good afternoon, sir.' Belatedly, as an after-thought, he included Jenny. 'Young lady.'

'You've had a message from the Chief of Police?'

'Indeed so, sir. He has requested I give you all the help I can. Walk this way.' He walked with his feet splayed apart like a duck. Jenny decided not to walk that way. The man opened a door and gestured for them to enter. 'The study. Perhaps this would be an appropriate place to begin?'

Jenny took out her notepad. Ken decided it was time to take the initiative. He pointed to himself and then to his companion. 'Detective Inspector Kenneth Jones and Detective Sergeant Jennifer Grace.' He decided to omit the 'acting'. It would have been more accurate but would have meant a loss of status in this man's eyes. 'I don't think we have your name?'

'Indeed not, sir. It was not my place to assume that you would wish to hear it. I am Carrington-Smithers. Amongst the staff and family here I am generally referred to as Smithers.'

Jenny needed to be sure that she was recording it accurately. 'But Carrington is your first name?' her pen was poised over the pad.

'Indeed not, miss.' He had made a point of looking at her left hand and the 'miss' was said with the slightest trace of a sneer, as if he was addressing a human rejected. 'My family name is Carrington-Smithers. It is double barrelled. I have other, Christian, names.'

Jenny was losing patience. 'And they would be?'

'James Carl. James after my great, great grandfather who was a member of Lord Palmerston's government' (Ken did a quick mental calculation and decided that if this were true, the man's ancestors were remarkably long lived) 'and Carl after my maternal grandfather, a leading German industrialist at the time of the Second World War. Alas, the allied victory led to his untimely demise and the loss of his fortune.'

Oddly, Jenny felt little sympathy! 'So you are known as James?'

Another smirk. 'Indeed not, my dear young lady. For a reason unknown to me, my parents always addressed me by my middle name.'

'So Carl, then?'

'Correct.'

Jenny wondered how long it would take to get any more information out of this stiff-necked apology for a human being if it had taken so long to get this far. Ken took over. 'And your role at the house is?'

'Many and varied, sir. Much responsibility has been placed upon my shoulders. First and foremost, I am the family's butler. I have been in service for more years than I care to remember. When I began, there would be a full staff of servants to tend to the needs of the house and garden. Alas, service is not regarded as worthwhile an occupation as it once was, Gradually the staffs shrank across the stately homes of England and it proved impossible to replace many of the servants The ones we have left are few in number, poorly trained and of…foreign extraction.'

'You have other roles?'

'Indeed, sir. I function as his lordship's valet when he is in the country.'

Jenny was quick to interject: 'He spends time abroad?'

The butler's voice dripped with sarcasm in response. 'Indeed not, miss. He regards

European countries to be too European for his taste and America too vulgar. When we say the country,' he gave her a look of contempt, 'we mean Dorset, of course.'

He was fortunate that Jenny did not have a taser or the excuse to use one. Ken felt for her and gave a gentle indication that he sympathised and he would ensure that they brought this rude man down. 'That's two roles, James.' He deliberately used his first name. despite the man's assertion that it was not customary, as a put down. 'You insinuated that you served several functions.'

The butler squirmed slightly, unwilling to give more information. 'If you pressed me, sir, I could confess to also being – how shall I put it? The estate manager. I look after his lordship's financial matters.'

Jenny was writing busily. 'Like an accountant?'

Contempt again. 'Accountancy, miss, is a trade. I am most definitely not a tradesperson. I am more of a chairman. A decision maker. I have no qualifications in accounting. My degree, from one of our oldest and most hallowed universities, is in Classical Studies.' His face distorted into what might have been a condescending smile. 'And yours is?'

'In the detection of smart arses.' Jenny snapped her notepad shut and turned to Ken. 'Shouldn't we start the interviews, boss?'

Ken was laughing inwardly. She had gone up in his estimation. 'Absolutely. Now James. If you don't mind, would you arrange for Jenny to meet and question the women who are in residence here?'

It was clear that Carrington-Smithers was disconcerted by this. 'Is she to do this alone, sir? Are you not going to accompany her?'

Ken gave him the brush off. 'That's not necessary. She's a very competent member of my team. Quite capable of conducting interviews on her own.'

'Quite so sir. So you will be…?' It was obvious that he was unhappy. He wanted them both in the same place so that he could keep an eye on them.

'I'll wait here,' Ken lied.

'Indeed so, sir. The estate's business dealings

are handled here in the study. Most of them are computerised now, of course. You are welcome to scrutinise them if you so wish.'

'Thank you. I just might do that.'

With obvious reluctance, the butler left the room, leading Jenny through the principal rooms towards the servants' quarters. Ken gazed at the computer screen. It had been left on, at an index page that would lead to the estate's financial dealings. He dismissed it. The computer would be taken away to be analysed, but the fact that it was on and the data were accessible meant, to his mind, that there was little here of interest. What was interesting was that there was no sign of any paperwork. The office was just too tidy. Ken was instantly suspicious. It looked as if it had been cleared of any incriminating evidence before they appeared. They had, after all, had prior knowledge of his arrival. This was annoying. If they had been allowed to get a search-warrant, they could have turned up without warning.

If his hunch was right, and paperwork had been removed, an attempt would probably have been made to destroy it. But how? And where?

18

The reception room was on the ground floor. No daylight came through the large bay window at one end. Thick blinds ensured that no-one could see in or out. The two sofas, on which the five girls were sitting, were faded and threadbare. The door to the right led to the stairs and the bedrooms. The other was the entrance from the street. Beside it was a desk and the woman sitting at it had a large cash box before her. Her task was to determine what service the men who entered wanted and take the money in advance. Then they could choose the girl they wanted. And they in turn were required to smile sweetly and look both willing and desirable. Any reluctance or petulance would result in a beating.

They were told that the minders who beat them were their protectors. A bell push next to each bed would summon help if a client threatened to hurt them. It was sort of reassuring. And they got a small amount of cash for each trick they pulled so that they could send money home, buy clothes and make-up. For two girls it was their first day on. Two customers sidled in, shiftily. They had docked that morning on a huge container ship. There was a whispered discussion with the woman at the door about services on offer and prices. She was fluent in several languages although her vocabulary was restricted to money and the words for sex acts. A wad of notes was passed over and the men turned to the girls, sitting in their underwear, trying to look seductive whilst feeling terrified. The door keeper pointed out the two new girls, advising the men that they were new and fresh. They were forced to stand and lead the two bearded sailors, dressed in soiled jeans and faded anoraks, upstairs.

Carrington-Smithers shuffled down the corridors trying to make it look as if he was not concerned that the DI had been left alone in the house. Jenny knew how important it was that Ken gained as much time as possible to conduct his search. She stopped at the bottom of the grand central staircase and asked its age. Her host forgot for a moment his anxiety and, flattered by her interest, explained that the mahogany balustrades were some of the finest in Europe and had been fitted in 1780 to a staircase that dated back to the late sixteenth century. Encouraged by her success, she pointed to a dark, over varnished portrait of a particularly unpleasant looking man in riding dress on a very depressed looking horse. 'Is that a family portrait?'

'Indeed so, miss. It is of the fourth earl, painted in celebration of his coming fourth in the Epsom Derby of 1823. Alas, he could not be painted riding the actual horse that had achieved this remarkable feat. He had flogged it rather too hard to the finishing line and, sad to say, it died before reaching the paddock.' It slowly dawned on him that Jenny was wasting his time. 'But I mustn't bore you with these matters, miss. You will be impatient to carry out your duties.' He led the way beyond the grand staircase. He opened a small door. A staircase led down from it. 'The servants' stairs, dear lady!' he announced, smugly. 'I have requested that the two ladies await us in the servants' hall.'

'Good.' And to make sure that he didn't go back to Ken: 'Lead the way!' It is greatly to Jenny's credit that, as he began to take the steps down to the service rooms, she did not give him a push that would have sent him crashing to the bottom.

Meanwhile, DI Jones had left the house by the servants' entrance at the rear and was searching for any sign of recent burning. Behind one of the glasshouses, he came across an incinerator. It was full of charred paper. Whoever had started the fire had done an excellent job. Most of the paper had turned to ash and disintegrated when touched. A few sheets were still almost whole but so blackened that no print was discernible. Ken had an evidence bag in his pocket. Taking great care, he transferred what he could to the plastic file. Whoever had incinerated them had not realised the skill of today's forensic scientists. Ken was sure that, under ultraviolet light, these sheets would reveal their secrets.

A quick walk back to the front of the house gave Ken the chance to conceal the evidence file in the car boot before re-entering the mansion by the back door. He strode rapidly through the public rooms back to the study, where he was found studying the computer when Jenny and the butler returned. He looked up as if he had been concentrating on the screen and was surprised to see them. 'How did it go?'

Jenny knew immediately, from the smile in Ken's eyes, that things had gone well for him, but it was not so for her. 'Bit of a setback, boss. The cook isn't the person we want. Her age and build are...well...they don't fit the description and she is always in the house making breakfast at the time the girl was seen. She told me that the maid has been going out for walks in the grounds after making up the fires and laying the morning table. I think she's the woman we want to interview, but I got nothing out of her!'

Carrington-Smithers smirked. 'She is of foreign extraction, sir and not the brightest specimen I'm afraid.' He seemed to find this amusing. 'Her command of the English language is almost non-existent. She will be of no use to you, I'm sorry to say.'

Ken was determined to undermine the man's smugness. 'Far from it. We'll take her to the station, find her country of origin and send out for an interpreter. Jenny, radio in to make sure that one is available as soon as we return.'

'Take her?' The butler was clearly rattled. He had assumed that the maid's lack of English would have led her to her being dismissed from the investigation. 'From the house?'

'Of course. She is a potential witness. The information she has could be of significant interest.' Ken smiled as if this should be self-explanatory.

Carrington-Smithers was struggling to accept what was happening. 'The young lady is under arrest?'

'Not at all. She is a possible witness, that's all.'

'I am exceedingly unhappy about allowing her to leave the premises. His lordship…'

'Would, I am sure, be happy to help the police with their investigation into such a serious case, as would any law-abiding citizen. The alternative,' he paused a second, giving the butler a hard stare, 'would leave him open to the offence of obstructing the police with their enquiries. And a possible prison sentence.'

Carrington-Smithers crumpled. 'I…er…if

you will excuse me, sir…and …dear lady…I will fetch the maid in question and escort her to your motor vehicle.'

'Thanks. And as a gesture of support, Jenny will go with you. After all, she may have questions that only Jenny could answer.'

The butler was unhappy. This would prevent him from trying to communicate the need for silence to the maid, by sign language presumably. He opened his mouth to object, on the ground that Jenny could not speak the maid's language, but before he could speak, Ken continued. 'We'll also be taking the office computer. We'll return it as soon as we've dismissed it from our enquiries.' Ken was on uncertain ground here, as he didn't have a search warrant, but the butler was so rattled by now that he had no time to object. 'And if you don't mind, we'll leave Jenny to escort the young lady on her own. I'd like you to take me to the gun room. We'll need to take all your shotguns. For forensic analysis.' The butler's mouth opened again, but no sound came out. 'Just to be sure that we can dismiss them from our enquiries!'

'Certainly sir if you'd just follow me.' And with a despairing glance at Jenny, as she disappeared towards the servants' stairs, the butler began to shuffle towards the back of the house with Ken in tow. They came to a strongroom door. The butler produced a bunch of keys from his pocket and two of them were needed to gain admission. Inside was a mini arsenal. Ken hoped that the owner had licences for them all, but left that question for another day. He walked purposefully to the shotguns, neatly racked along the far wall. 'Have any of these been out recently?'

Carrington-Smithers looked shifty. 'They are kept for the shoots, when his lordship's aristocratic friends gather here for the pheasants. They are not in daily use, I can assure you, sir.'

'Has there been a recent shoot?'

The butler looked shocked. 'The shooting season ends at the end of January. Surely you know that?'

Ken walked up to the guns. They were all covered with a light film of dust, except one. 'This one's been used recently.'

Carrington-Smithers looked, if possible, even shiftier. 'His lordship likes…on occasion…when he walks the estate…very rarely…to carry a shotgun…for purposes of a more ritual nature…to establish his…err…status with the villagers…to deter any possible trespass…'

Ken removed the gun from the rack and swung it round towards the cowering man. He had no intention of attacking him and he assumed it was not loaded, but the butler pressed against the wall as if in danger of his life. 'And has his lordship been on one of his armed prowls this week?'

His interviewee seemed to be in danger of collapsing to the floor. 'I really wouldn't like to say, sir. I don't follow his every movement!'

'Three mornings ago?'

'It is indeed possible sir.' He seemed to reflect for a moment. 'In fact, I can confirm that he did. I noticed it especially because he normally carries an unloaded gun – for effect you know. But on this occasion, he took with him a small quantity of ammunition. I thought at the time that this was very unusual.'

Ken walked to the strongroom door, gun in hand. 'We'll be taking this to the lab for tests.'

'If you think it's best. Sir.'

221

The internet was humming around Bishop Farthing now that the police had revealed the identity of the body. The representatives of the national media had drifted away because there had been no salacious developments. The body of a young woman, sparsely clad, is a subject of national scrutiny for weeks and every detail must be squeezed out of the story in the public interest. It may even lead to demonstrations on the streets, all night vigils and questions in parliament to the home secretary: but, oddly, the death of a man, or an older woman, slips out of the public consciousness as fast and as slippery as a Prime Minister's indiscretions.

But in the village of Bishop Farthing the truth was proving even more shocking than cattle rustling or tractor theft. Almost all wanted to send their condolences to Elyse, even those who had never really known or met her. She was suddenly one of theirs. An impressive display of bouquets began to form along her fence. Brightly coloured and oddly inappropriate, some with caring and mis-spelt messages of love and sympathy (a few from children had forlorn soft toys attached) they were gradually fading and going limp, in tune with the level of national concern.

Almost no-one actually called on her. It is so difficult to know what to say in these circumstances. The cowardly assumption is that she would not want to be troubled with visitors at this time – would surely prefer to be alone. So Elyse, who yearned for company, had only her sister to console her. There was not even a vicar to call at the house. The living of Bishop Farthing had been without an incumbent priest since the departure of the last, with his close friend the sexton, in somewhat scandalous circumstances. And so, Elyse and Angela were left to struggle alone not only with grief, but also with the financial problems caused by unexpected death. Alec's bank accounts had to be closed. His standing orders, including his annual payment to the Tamiya Members' Club, had to be cancelled. He had died young without a will so there were probate problems. Without Angela's help, Elyse would have simply given up. It was just too much. And that was before the insurance details were sorted out. And his private pension.

19

On their way back to HQ, Ken and Jenny, with their bewildered passenger, drove over Bulbarrow Hill. From the summit, they had an awesome vista of North Dorset spread beneath them. Endless small fields formed a rolling chequerboard pattern of greens, browns and yellows. Endless hedgerows, scattered with trees, formed darker green boundary lines that seemed to follow no clear pattern – and, in fact, didn't. Small hamlets and church towers punctuated the view, small enough to look like tiny models, too tiny to ever house people. Jenny breathed in as she gazed across the landscape, designated as an area of outstanding natural beauty, and it was obvious why. She couldn't help but feel romantic as she thrilled to it, but they were on duty and, with a passenger in the car, she didn't even lean against Ken's arm to assuage the warm glow in her heart.

Twenty-five minutes later they pulled into the car park and Ken switched off the blue flashing lights. An interpreter was waiting for them inside. She was fluent in most Eastern European languages and the first task was to find out which one their charge spoke. She drew a blank with Polish and Hungarian. The interpreter sighed. She was going to have to try one of the tongues in which she had less confidence. She swept back her hair, auburn with streaks of grey and smoothed her hands down her tweed skirt.

'Buna ziua,' she tried. On hearing this the young woman became agitated, nodding and speaking too rapidly for the interpreter, Paulette, to follow. Then the words became clearer.

'Am fost arestat?' she repeated over and over again, clearly distressed.

Paulette reassured her that no, she was not under arrest and began to translate Ken's questions into Romanian.

Yes, she had been on the edge of the woods that fateful day, three mornings ago. She had gone to meet someone. Jenny walked swiftly to the incident board and unpinned a picture of

Alec taken from Facebook before he became a corpse. She showed it to the Romanian. Yes, she nodded, and then clutched at the photograph and began to weep. Jenny reached for the picture nervously, fearing that the tears would ruin it, but Ken gestured to her to leave it. They could make another copy.

Through Paulette, Ken asked if she had been in a sexual relationship with Alec. No, there was no romantic attraction. He was, she told them, a nice man who had wanted to ask her about why she was there, but they could not understand each other. 'A vrut sa ma ajute!'

Jenny was curious. 'Why was she there? How had she come to be working in the house?'

The interpreter struggled with the question, but finally made the young woman, whose name they discovered was Rina, understand what they wanted. Paulette made a mental note that the name means devotion and purity in Romanian but doubted that it was relevant here. And the more she discovered, the more true that seemed. Rina told them that she had been smuggled into the country. Men who seemed wealthy and well connected had convinced her family that they could find her an excellent post with a wealthy

British household as a nanny or au pair. She would have a good future, probably marry a rich Englishman and be able to send money home to Romania.

Reality was very different. She was trapped in a large house and forced to become a sex worker. Ken looked up in surprise. Rina was not an obvious candidate for the work. Her hair was long, lank, and thin. Her face was pockmarked from childhood chicken pox and her very pale skin showed signs of acne. Despite the beatings, she told them, she had refused the work and had been sent, in disgrace, to work for his lordship. Ken asked if she had been paid. The interpreter struggled and had to refer to her phone for one of the words, but finally asked, 'Cat castigi?'

Rina's total confusion told its own story. She had a room and her keep. That was it. She had been little more than a domestic slave.

Ken sensed that there was a part of this story that didn't add up. If Alec and Rina weren't having an affair and had so much difficulty understanding each other, why were they meeting regularly? What was drawing them together, at breakfast time, deep in the wood? He asked Paulette to probe her, but the more she asked, the more upset the Romanian became. Ken was increasingly concerned that there was more to this than some casual bonding. He sat opposite her and stared at her, slightly threateningly, although it was against his nature to bully vulnerable women. Here, though, something was being concealed and he needed to know what it was. It could be a critical piece of evidence. He spoke to Paulette, who was behind him, without turning his head from Rina.

'Tell her that she could be in serious trouble if she doesn't tell the truth.' Paulette jabbered away in Romanian to the poor woman, doing her best to make this clear. Ken saw the fear in Rina's eyes deepen.

'Tell her we know that she was meeting Alec for a reason. She must tell us everything.' Again Paulette did her best to convey this to Rina. She looked even more distressed, waving her hands in agitation. But no more information came from her.

'Tell her this. Keeping evidence from the police is a serious offence. If she doesn't come clean to us, she is facing a long term in prison!'

Both Gina and Jenny, who could both hear

this, looked slightly alarmed. This was a side of Ken that they had never seen before.

It did the trick. Rina began to shake violently with sobs. In between outpourings of tears, she began to utter words and phrases that were some kind of confession. Paulette listened carefully, without interrupting the words that burst between sobs from Rina's lips – just occasionally jotting down notes on a pad so she kept the thread. Finally, as the words failed Rina and she gave way only to tears, Paulette took her hand. She spoke softly, reassuringly. 'Va multumesc. Esti o fata buna.' The team gathered round in the office had no idea what this meant, but it seemed to have the right effect, Rina's sobs reduced in intensity. Jenny handed her a bunch of tissues and she wiped her eyes and blew her nose, still very distressed.

Paulette glanced at her notes and then updated the team. 'They were meeting because Rina wanted to send money back to her family in Romania. Her father had been killed during a Communist putsch when she was very young. There were just her, her mother and grandmother at home. But they had no means of support. They were relying on Rina sending money from her work in England.

She had met Alec when he visited the house on business. He had talked nicely to her, even though she couldn't understand much of what he said. She knew he was something to do with money. Somehow she indicated to him that she wanted – needed - to send money and showed him an address. He promised to help her. She would meet him at the edge of the wood and pass him an envelope with money in. She knew from…from the messages that she got from home, that he was doing it for her.'

This made sense – as far as it went. Geoff called across from his desk. 'That figures, boss! It explains the money transactions that he was making to Romania. All for fairly small amounts!'

Ken looked bemused. 'Yes, but where was the money coming from? Even though they were only forty or fifty pounds – is that what you said?' Geoff nodded. 'She wasn't getting paid.' He turned to Paulette, 'Ask her where the money came from.'

Paulette was still struggling. 'If we go through this again, I'll need to bring a dictionary!

Romanian isn't one of my strengths. There aren't too many of them in Dorset!' Using a few carefully chosen words and some sign language, she managed to get the question across. Once again, Rina showed signs of extreme distress. Eventually, as she glanced about the room as if looking for an escape route, she confessed that she had taken the money, picked it up around the house, even taken small amounts from the safe when she saw it open. Ken told Paulette to reassure her that she wouldn't be in trouble for it. The amounts were small and far less than she should have been paid, anyway.

For now, he had more important leads to follow. First, he had a hunch about the house she had been taken to when she arrived in England. He asked Geoff to use street view to download pictures of the houses that were part of the estate, the houses that were bringing in far more than student's accommodation should. 'It turns out there are more than I first realised, boss. The estate owned numerous properties in the Southampton and Portsmouth areas. The first four were of principal interest because of their size. But there are many others only slightly smaller. They own a couple of streets! It's all right for some, right boss?'

'Is the same thing happening with them all? A sudden big increase in rental income?'

'Yes boss. But it doesn't tie in with the estate accounts. The rent shown there has stayed more or less the same over the last three years. The extra money's being syphoned off somewhere. I'll keep on trying to track it down.'

'Good man. In the meantime, concentrate on pictures of the first four. If she was being held, it would probably be in one of those.'

Geoff produced four photos of large, rundown buildings; the ground floor windows boarded up. Ken showed each in turn to Rina and Paulette asked if she recognised any of them.

She didn't. She'd had little chance to observe the outside of the building. She was, however, able to confirm that there had been no natural light downstairs, where the clients entered. Ken was far from sure how all this hung together, but he had heard enough to realise that these buildings needed to be investigated. Nick was instructed to contact the Hampshire vice officers. Tomorrow morning, Ken and his team would join them in a series of raids. But in the meantime, what had Rina seen in the wood that fateful morning?

It was clear that both Paulette and Rina needed a break. The strain was telling on both. He told the whole team to take half an hour off, get sandwiches and coffee, stretch their legs. He needed to stay and sort out his thoughts. Jenny said she'd get him something and he suggested a couple of different fillings in case they didn't have his first choice. He offered some money, but she said they'd settle later. Now he was alone, in the empty office. He still couldn't go into the DI's room at the end. Longbottom's things were still in there. He had not retired officially yet. It wouldn't do to use it, even though he could do with it. He went to the window and stared out into the carpark below. His phone rang. It was Sheila.

'I've got some news, Ken. You're not going to like it. I'm afraid.'

Ken was not expecting this. He was slightly bewildered. 'About the case?'

'The body in the woods? No. It's more about…us.'

'Us?'

'Ken, I tried to break away, just like I promised. It was difficult to talk it through, Harold just never wanted to discuss it. If I tried, he would just change the subject and refuse to listen.'

'I can't tell you what to do.'

'No.'

'But if you really want to end it – and I believe you do, of course – you've got to be firm, Sheila. He can't go on just ignoring you!'

'I was. I wrote it all down. How it wasn't working for me. That the difference in our ages was just too great. I sent it on the internal mail system, to make sure that his wife wouldn't see it. I wanted to make a clean break. I honestly did, Ken!'

He began to sweat. Something about this didn't sound right. She had said he wouldn't like the news. So what had gone wrong? He was hesitant. 'Sheila…that sounds just right…Even considerate…'

'He turned up last night. On my doorstep.'

'What?'

'With a suitcase. He said there'd been a hell

of a row. His wife had found out about us.'

'How?'

'And she'd thrown him out.'

'Bloody hell!'

'And he'd nowhere else to go…'

'Jesus, Sheila! What about hotels?'

'Ken, I couldn't. I'm partly responsible, after all.'

His mind was working overtime. 'Don't you think it's a bit suspicious? Farfetched? What a bloody coincidence! You send him a note ending it and it's the same day his wife throws him out!'

'He says he never got the note. It's still in his in-tray!'

'And you believe him? Sheila!'

He saw Jenny enter the office with his snack and ended the call. He was furious. He had been angry at Sheila's insistence on delay after their evening at her flat. But now… The fact that her boss had taken her from him made him want her more and what he saw as her stupidity in accepting this feeble story made him seethe. He grabbed loose sheets of paper from his desk, screwed them up and threw them, forcefully into the bin on the other side of the room. Jenny looked at him in consternation. 'You all right boss?'

'Don't ask. Bloody, bloody woman!'

Jenny had enough female intuition to work out who he was referring to. She decided to let the matter drop. Very quietly, she passed over his meal deal sandwich and sat to eat hers at her desk many metres away.

Paulette escorted Rina back into the interview room and Ken switched on the tape recorder. They were getting to the crux of the interview. He forced the desolate thoughts from his mind and concentrated on what he had to do. First, he gave Rina a welcoming smile to put her at ease. 'How is she, Paulette?'

'Very nervous. She still thinks that she is in serious trouble.'

Ken realised that he needed to do something to reassure her. 'Tell her that we realise that she is in the country illegally. But if she helps us, we'll do our best to ensure that she isn't deported. And there's no question of prison. We'll put her in witness protection – a secure bedsit.'

Paulette did her best to translate this into Romanian. 'But we can't guarantee that she'll be able to stay here?'

Ken slowly shook his head. 'We'll recommend that she stays. That she's done a service to the country. But we'll be dealing with the Home Office. You can never tell.'

Paulette spoke softly to Rina, trying to sound reassuring, but the smile faded from her face.

'Ask her who she saw when she went to the wood that day. Did she see Ken?'

Paulette asked – with one or two gestures to help where her vocabulary was lacking. Once Rina understood, the words poured from her and she was clearly upset at the memory. 'No. She had gone with another packet of money for him to send home, but she couldn't see him anywhere.'

This wasn't promising. Ken tried again. 'Did she see anyone? Who else was there?'

Rina wriggled uncomfortably in her chair. She was obviously reluctant to tell. Ken prompted her. 'What about the butler?

Carrington-Smithers? Did she see him?'

Rina shook her head. 'But you did see someone?' Jenny was almost ready to turn off the recorder. This could be interpreted as leading the witness, but before she could touch it, words came out of Rina in a rush.

Paulette showed sign of distress as she struggled to keep up. Then: 'She is terrified of her employer…'

'His lordship?'

'He – how can I put it – gropes her.'

'Has he made her sleep with him?'

'I don't think so. She hasn't said so. He just touches her whenever he passes her. He's well into his eighties, isn't he? Maybe that's all he can manage!'

'She's afraid of him – is that why she's reluctant to say who she saw? Was it her employer?'

Paulette stroked Rina's arm reassuringly. She spoke softly to her. Eventually Rina nodded. 'For the benefit of the recording, the witness nods to indicate that yes, her employer was at the scene.' Ken pressed on. 'Was he carrying anything? A shotgun, perhaps?'

Again, Rina was reluctant to speak, but once she understood the question she nodded and spoke the international language of gunfire: 'Bang bang!'

Ken's heart leapt. 'You heard gunshots?'

Paulette translated; Rina nodded.

'For the purpose of the recording, the witness has nodded. Rina, this is important. Did your employer fire the shots? He was the one with a gun. Did you see him fire it?'

Again Paulette put this to Rina. She wasn't certain, but she thought yes, he had fired the gun. 'And did you see Alec at all? Anywhere?'

When she said no, Ken was not surprised. It would have been impossible to see the body, face down in the undergrowth, from where she was standing. He would have been already dead. It was time to give Rina a well-deserved rest in a safe location and call in the full team.

It took less than half an hour to bring them all together, Ken stood by the board with the pictures and maps. There was now a plan of Southampton docks with the houses pinned that belonged to the estate. They had added a photo of Rina and one of his lordship from Reuters. Photos of the house from the air and a picture of the shotgun that Alec had brought back completed the display.

Ken sensed that they were close to solving the mystery, but he was aware that they didn't, as yet, have a convincing motive for the killing. However, he was upbeat as he addressed his team. They had grown increasingly confident of his leadership and were certainly up for it. There was an alertness that had rarely been present when Longbottom had called them together. And they had heard of how their new leader had dealt with the two yobs who had assaulted one of their number. Maybe Ken's reaction to the attack on Jenny had been slightly over the top, but it was the sort of response that gained respect among fellow officers. They were all more than ready to support him and go the extra mile, if necessary.

'Right guys, listen up! Here's where we've got to. First, we've got a possible murder weapon. Nick, what word have we got from forensics on the shotgun I retrieved from the manor?'

'They're still running tests, boss — but it's looking good. It was the right calibre, and the scorings look as if they're a match. It's been recently fired and there's a clear set of prints.'

'Any ID?'

'They don't match any in our data base, unfortunately, so it's someone without a previous record.'

'Just one set? No-one else's?'

Nick shook his head. 'No boss. But it looks as if we've found the gun. They're already ninety percent positive that it fired the fatal shot.'

'So we have the weapon. And we have two witnesses who place it in the hands of his lordship. The butler has stated that he was the one who took it out that morning, And the maid, Rina, saw him with it at the scene, She heard gunshots at the time we estimate the killing took place and the two who found the body, Peter and Beth, verify that the maid was in the field next to the woods just after they heard the shots, so its all looking fairly watertight.

'It's not done and dusted yet. Two problems. One: it could be difficult to bring his lordship in for questioning. Apparently, he's in

Westminster, at the House of Lords, and there are important debates going on. In any case, being who he is, it's going to be highly sensitive. We don't want any of this going to the press at this stage, is that clear? No word of this outside of this room?'

There were nods from everyone, even from those who had lucrative contacts with journalists. They wouldn't let their new boss down.

Jenny was unhappy about the sensitivity of speaking to the suspect. 'Do you mean that he'll be protected, boss? By his position and his money?' She would object strongly to this. It went directly against her socialist principles.

'Not if I have anything to do with it. But here's a heads up. I've already had a gentle word from the Chief Constable. We need to be careful. Not rush into this. We'll need to have our facts absolutely certain.'

'Right boss,'

Now for the second problem. If he did shoot him — and that looks likely — we have no motive. Why would he do it? The only lead we have is a financial one. It looks as if some of the properties owned by the estate are suddenly bringing in suspiciously high rental income. It could mean a link with organised crime – via vice or drugs or both, There's some evidence from emails that Alec Bartle, who was their accountant, was starting to ask questions. But was that enough to have him killed? And if so, would his lordship have become an assassin? Something isn't right. Geoff – any more progress on the bank statements?'

'Not much more, boss. Except I can't find out where the excess money goes. The money in the business accounts has stayed the same as it was two years ago. But we know the income from the lettings has shot up. It's just dropping down a hole somewhere.'

'There was that business with the charred papers that someone was trying to destroy. Any more on that?'

'They've only just been sent to forensics, boss. Nothing yet. I'll let you know as soon as they send anything through.'

'Thanks Geoff. Do that. Gina – anything useful from the television appeal?'

'A stream of useless drivel, sarge – I mean

boss. The wood is so isolated it doesn't seem anyone saw anything – except for the people we've already been in contact with. These folk in Bishop Farthing though! Well. There's someone called Trevor who wants to know if we want him to form a vigilante group. A woman with the unlikely name of Fifi is with the fairies. She called to say that she thinks she saw a man last night crawling on his hands and knees past her house. But she says it might have been a large dog. A woman who seems to be a religious maniac is reporting everyone in the village for offences ranging from adultery to having a noisy dog. Half of them are crackers!'

'Well thanks for all you've done, Gina. Keep on with it just in case something useful comes up! Nick, chase up forensics and keep an eye on the budget. Try to keep their costs at a reasonable level. Right team. You've got your jobs for tomorrow. I'll be going to Southampton with Jenny first thing to join up with Hampshire vice to raid a number of properties to find out why they're suddenly worth thousands of pounds a week! Okay gang, Get some rest. I want you fresh and alert tomorrow!'

Gina half raised a hand. 'We're going to the

pub for a goodnight drink first boss. Want to join us?'

'Can't I'm afraid. The A.C.C. wants me to call her. I think our interest in his lordship has begun to stir up trouble!'

There was a chorus of 'Good night boss!' 'Good luck!' as the team left, leaving only Jenny standing beside him as he picked up the phone.

'Jones?'

'Yes, ma'am.'

'What's the situation with his lordship?'

Ken could sense the chill coming from the other end of the line. The Assistant Chief Constable was rumoured not to have been born, but rather carved by her parents out of a block of ice. She had a face as hard as granite and eyes that would kill a small mammal at thirty paces. She had got where she was by having a backbone of steel and destroying any rivals with her withering brand of sarcasm. She was never seen except in full police uniform and hat – to give her extra height. It was said that she slept in it. Some people have so much charisma that when they enter a room everyone notices. When A.C.C Jean Crossley enters a room, everyone freezes. She was head girl at her grammar school and captain of the hockey team. She was certainly born to lead, but no-one is sure where.

'We want to bring him in for questioning over the Bartle killing.'

'The grounds?'

'We have a witness who saw him at the scene at the time of the shooting. Two who testify that he was carrying a shotgun; and forensics are confident that it was the gun that fired the fatal shot. There is only one set of prints on the gun. They're not on our data base, but we don't have his lordship's prints on file.'

'You'll need to get his prints then.'

'Ideally, yes.'

'Not ideally yes. Just yes. You'll need to find some way of getting them without accusing him of anything. This whole business will have to be handled with kid gloves.'

'I understand, ma'am.'

'You're very new to be tackling this, Jones. If you pull this off, it'll be a feather in your cap. Bugger it up and your career's probably over.'

'No pressure then, ma'am,' Ken responded, drily.

'The only good thing about this is - that cretin Longbottom isn't in charge. He'd have got us all put in the tower. I've alerted the Royal Protection Squad at the Met and filled them in. They'll pick his lordship up straight from his grace and favour apartment first thing in the morning and bring him direct to you. I want to make it clear, Jones, that he'll think he is helping police with their enquiries – not a bloody suspect. Don't charge him with anything unless you're bloody sure it'll stick. No publicity – at all – under any circumstances, got that?'

'Yes, ma'am. I've already warned my team to contact no-one about this.'

'Well, at least you've got some bloody thing right. And don't do anything – at all – without clearing it with me first!'

'Understood, ma'am.'

'Goodnight, Jones. And God help us all.'

'Night ma'am.'

Ken went to the gym before home. He needed to work off numerous frustrations.

20

Back in Bishop Farthing, Peter was in Beth's bed, cuddled up to her. She had her back to him and they lay together like two spoons. He listened to her steady breathing and knew that she had not yet fallen asleep. He was long, over six feet, and curling up like this kept his toes from sticking out of the bed. Beth was five foot four. She felt sometimes like a child in his arms. But she was not a child. He had learnt to respect her intellect as well as loving her. She had not had a university education, it's true, but was no worse for that. She was a quick learner and more than made up in common sense for anything she may have lacked in scholarship. Beth was quiet and sensible. She didn't wear ridiculous pointed heels because they were fashionable or spend huge amounts of money on perfume or make-up that she didn't need. She was quiet and pretty, everything that Peter longed for in a partner.

He was shy and awkward in women's company. It had taken many months to rustle up the courage to speak to Beth – and when it had finally happened, it had been the result of a ridiculous misunderstanding. He still went pale when he remembered it – it could so easily have been the end of their relationship before it had begun – if she had not been so understanding. His greatest regret was that his one clumsy attempt to propose, while they were on holiday together last year, had been unsuccessful. Beth wasn't sure that their lifestyles were compatible. She needed music, companionship, conversation, a pretty and comfortable home. He needed quiet and solitude when he was working – no distractions.

They loved each other but rationed their time together. He would see her twice a week – rarely more. They would spend the night together: usually at her house. It was something, but not enough. Because what they had seen in the wood had changed things. It is not possible to go for a quiet early morning stroll in the romance of a deep bluebell wood with someone who is precious to you and find a dead body in the undergrowth and not be affected by it. The experience had drawn them closer; intensified their need for comfort and companionship. Since that morning he had spent every night with her. They were consolation and security for each other. And even though it had meant only four nights in a row, it was enough to make him realise that this was what he wanted, more than anything.

'Beth...'

'Uhmm?' She was almost asleep.

'I know that you value your independence. I know that you need your own space and I do respect that.'

'Uhmm?'

'But what if...I know it's difficult...suppose we still had our separate homes – we could retreat to during the day sometimes - but we could be like this every night...together...loving each other...and I do love you, so very much – you know that don't you..? Do you think there's a chance that could work? And we could well – if you'd have me...get married, perhaps..?'

It was the longest and most romantic speech he had ever made. He lay with bated breath, waiting for her answer. Had he pushed things too far? Had he got it wrong again?

Beth rolled over and looked straight at him. Then she inclined her head towards him and kissed him gently on the lips. 'Okay.'

The next morning, the car was cruising along the A27 towards Southampton with Ken at the wheel and Jenny at his side. A squad of officers followed in a police van, both vehicles flashing blue lights but not using their sirens. At the rendezvous they'd join up with similar units from the Hampshire force and be given their targets

Jenny glimpsed a group of New Forest ponies munching grass beyond the low fence that protected them from the speeding traffic on the dual carriageway. A dark green patch of woodland flashed by as they passed a sign to the Rufus Stone, claimed to mark the spot where King William the Second was killed in a hunting accident. Jenny breathed in the fresh, clean smelling air. This was so far removed from the job they were about to undertake, the breaking up of a vice ring and the release of girls forced into prostitution.

Jenny relaxed back in her seat and looked across at Ken. His profile was almost Roman. He had a strong chin and nose, dark eyebrows and eyes that concentrated unblinking on the road ahead. She was a devout Christian but had inherited from her mother in Jamaica a religious belief that stretched into the supernatural. Her mother was convinced people could be reincarnated, if they still had scores to settle in this world. Could it be true? She had heard of a case that had baffled scientists. A girl in York had begun to speak a language no-one recognised and woke screaming night after night, dreaming that she was on fire.

Experts in linguistics eventually realised that she was speaking a medieval form of Hebrew – a language she could never have heard. Under hypnosis, she revealed that she was a Jewess, taking refuge in York castle. Further research revealed that all this had actually happened, in 1190 AD, when the entire Jewish community in York was attacked and killed in an anti-Semitic riot. The only explanation seemed to be that she was remembering something that had happened to her in a former life.

Jenny wondered, idly, if she and Ken had been together in a former life. Maybe Ken had been a wealthy Roman and she one of his slaves. Or maybe she had been a wealthy lady in

Victorian England and Ken had been her gamekeeper… She pushed naughty thoughts out of her mind as they approached the rendezvous point. She was no Barbie after all and if that was the sort of woman that Ken wanted…well, he wasn't for her any more than she was for him.

They pulled into the rendezvous site and lined up along with five other task force groups – one for each building they were targeting. Each small convoy was joined by two armed officers in case of trouble. Only then were they given – over the radio – their target destination. This meant there was no possibility of a leak forewarning any of the organised crime groups that they hoped to hit.

All six set off together, racing down the M271, blue lights flashing and sirens blaring. Other traffic moved over into the inside lane to give way and they reached the major roundabout at the end of the motorway in seconds. Passers-by looked on in wonder as the convoy swung onto Millbrook Road and headed for the docks. Two huge container ships had just arrived and were beginning to unload. Further on, around the cruise terminals, three gigantic cruise ships were docked and there was a long queue of resultant traffic, passengers eager to depart mingling with supply lorries restocking the liners. The police vehicles squeezed between them and vehicles moving in the opposite direction before splitting up to their predetermined destinations.

Ken and Jenny led their force off the main road and onto the minor ones around the football stadium. There was a mixture of housing – some dating back to the late eighteenth century, some built after the second world war to replace property that was damaged by bombs and industrial sites that cropped up in between like bad teeth. None of it seemed to be owner occupied. This was bedsit land or student rooms. They swung past the football ground, over a level crossing and screeched to a halt outside a tall Edwardian tenement. The façade was crumbling. Cement was cracking off the walls. The window paint was peeling and some of the panes were cracked. This was a building that had stood unloved for many years and, rather than complain, was simply surrendering to its fate and very slowly sinking into a state in which it would be uninhabitable.

Ken deployed his forces. Three of his strongest officers were deployed to the back to trap any who sought escape by the rear. The rest were divided in two. The first team, all male, were the crash team who would force entry and make the initial arrests. The second team would follow behind. Mainly female officers, their role would be vital if it turned out that there were women inside.

Geoff was poised at the main door, holding the battering ram. Ken motioned to him to pause for a moment. He stood next to him and shouted, 'Armed police! We're coming in!' and turned the handle. The door opened without the need of force. He led the first team in. They wore heavy body armour and helmets to protect the face. A formidable sight, even without the two armed officers in the vanguard.

The door opened to a large entrance hall. A woman was standing behind a desk, looking alarmed. She had shot to her feet as the police entered and her chair had fallen back behind her. The only other furniture consisted of two faded and sagging sofas. On one, two young women were cowering in terror. They struggled to cover their bodies with their hands to disguise the fact that they were wearing only the skimpiest of undergarments. Ken took the first cohort through to the stairs and on to the first floor, leaving the women officers in the rear to deal with the woman and girls.

Three rooms and a bathroom. The bathroom was filthy, the walls riddled with damp and the basin stained brown. The bedrooms were far from romantic boudoirs. The wallpaper was old, featuring nicotine-stained flower patterns from the fifties, yellowed with age: the ceilings, yellow ochre from tobacco smoke. The paper was peeling off the window wall, where cold and damp had done its worst. The only light filtered in through cracks in the wood planking that filled the windowpanes and ensured that escape via that route was impossible. The smell of dirty bedlinen was masked by the overpowering stench of cheap perfume. In each bedroom, a man was hurriedly trying to dress, falling over in his effort to pull on his trousers and run. In each room a pathetic, pale, skinny young woman tried to wrap herself in the filthy bed sheets.

Ken moved on to the top floor, leaving officers behind to deal with the 'clients' and put the fear of God in them. The girls were instructed to dress and were accompanied by women officers to safety. On the stairs, he passed Doina, who huddled against the wall in fright. Looking into her eyes, he saw for one terrible fleeting moment the fear and helplessness he had he had once glimpsed in the face of his own mother and fury gripped him as he leapt up the remaining steps. On the top floor, three further rooms. Two were bedrooms with the doors open, ready for the two remaining girls they'd found in reception. The door to the final room was closed.

Ken was looking for the pimps who ran the show. He heard scuffling behind the door. 'Open the door! Police!'

Silence.

Ken tried the handle. The door was locked. He put his shoulder to it. The door was old and flimsy. It had never been built for defence. And Ken was fit and strong. The wood splintered and the door crashed open.

There were two men inside. Both were dark, with black stubble on their faces. They wore black pants and white open-necked shirts, much smarter - and better quality - than the clothes they allowed the girls they exploited. On one wall, bunk beds. A small safe and cooking equipment. Two easy chairs and a desk made up the rest of the furniture. Piles of notes neatly stacked on the desktop. Divided into different currencies – mainly stacks of dollars and euros. Some sterling. Others that Ken recognised as Turkish or Chinese currency – others that he had never seen before.

The two men had already reacted to his arrival. One was yanking open the window. Ken decided to leave him for the moment. There was no fire escape. The room was high up, far too far to escape from by jumping. The other was a different matter.

He was the heavier of the two and more nimble. He was diving for a drawer in the desk. It was immediately clear to Ken that it contained something that he would use to defend himself. It could be a knife, or, worse, a gun. He didn't wait to find out. Ken lunged forward and pushed the top of the desk hard into the man's stomach. He grunted and fell back. The detective leapt over the desk and swung a fist at the man's head. The abuser reached up to take

Ken by the throat, but he was winded and disorientated. At this point, Ken should have called for assistance and held the man down until others from his team arrived and could help to restrain and handcuff the suspect.

But that's not what happened. As Ken looked down at the miserable example of human scum that lay beneath him, a red mist came over him. For a few seconds he was not an adult, a protector of the public, an enforcer of law and order. He was a small child, huddled behind his bedroom door. From downstairs, he could hear again his mother's screams and cries as his father thrust his fists into her. He had taken out his frustration and anger on his wife, time and time again. Ever since he had lost his job and spent what money he had not on his family but on drink and drugs, he had vented his rage on the only person in the world who cared for him. And she, bewildered and lost, had accepted this as something she, in some incomprehensible way, deserved.

Every morning after, as his father lay in a drunken stupor on the sofa downstairs, the small boy would sneak into his mother's bed and hug her, as if his tiny arms wrapped around her would keep her safe. And he swore that he would never willingly accept that men could use their strength or power to abuse women. And so Ken lost it. The pimp cried out in pain as he thudded fist after fist into his head. Then Ken staggered to his feet and aimed two kicks at the man's midriff. His boot sank into the area below the rib cage with satisfying ferocity. The beaten man made no effort to defend himself. Oddly, it seemed that he was prepared to take the beating, even if it resulted in his death, without any protest. He made one strangled grunt and blood spilt from his mouth. Only then did he lose consciousness.

Ken regained some kind of self-possession at last and gazed at the body at his feet in confusion. He looked up. Jenny and Geoff were at the door, staring at him in disbelief. Jenny was the first to find her voice.

'Evading arrest, sir. Justifiable force.'

Ken walked to the far side of the desk and looked in the drawer. He took a tissue from his pocket and pulled an evil looking knife from within, where it had lain half hidden under several more stashes of bank notes. Jenny pulled on plastic gloves and took it from him, without speaking. She went to the body on the floor and wrapped his fingers around the blade. She looked up. 'Better call an ambulance, sir. He's breathing.'

Only then did Ken remember the second man – leaner and fitter – who had exited via the third-floor window before he could reach him. Was there some way of escaping from there? Had they preprepared for this and attached a rope ladder or some way of accessing a drain pipe? The window was wide open. Ken put his head and shoulders through and looked down. The second pimp had been even more unlucky than the first. The yard below was in deep shadow. The man could not have seen the iron railings when he launched himself out. His body was limp as a rag doll. Skewered on the spikes of the black iron fence below.

Little more than an hour later, Chief Super Forsythe was leading the debrief at Hampshire Police HQ. He was wearing his full uniform, including the hat, despite the warm sunshine pouring into the room. He had a face that you could believe had never been graced by a smile, even as a child. Deep lines of worry and pain seemed to be etched onto it. Yet today he was as close to looking pleased as he had ever been. The operation had gone well.

'Firstly, let me sum up the progress we made today. Each of you will be fully aware of the success of your individual aspect of the raids, but it is my task now to share the full picture with you all. Six houses were raided, all identified for us by our colleagues at Dorset CID as a result of an investigation they are currently carrying out. Three of the properties turned out to be brothels, as expected. The women involved were all illegal immigrants from Eastern Europe and have been taken into custody for their own safe keeping. A total of eighteen women, some of them no more than girls, were involved. Three of whom seem to have been in charge.

'Of the other three houses, one was a small two-bedroom property away from the docks. Here we uncovered a massive drug haul – more than twenty kilos of cocaine along with countless uppers, downers and assorted inbetweeners!' His audience laughed politely at this extremely poor attempt at humour. The mood was generally good. They knew things had gone well.

'The other two houses were acting as storage for a large range of fraudulent goods. Cases of watches that claimed to be Rolex, stashes of clothing with expensive labels, electronic goods with high end tags. All cheap imitations of course, but worth several million on the open market.

'We're tracking the packages now to ascertain how they arrived in the country. I suspect they've been smuggled in from China in containers. Luckily, some of them were still unopened and had consignment notes attached. This means we can identify the routes they took and the actual ships they came in on. With luck, we may have smashed a major smuggling operation.

'Arrests have been few. Three of the houses contained no people at all. We have to suspect that there was some kind of advance warning – a leak. This is the only dark side to the day. There will be profoundly serious consequences if we find that anyone on the force gave any sort of tip off about today.' The mood darkened slightly. 'Arrests were made, however, at two of the properties being used as brothels. Two men were detained at target three, even though the suspects made desperate attempts to escape. We have the good work to thank of Task Force Three, who ensured that every line of escape was covered and used tasers to bring the men down as they attempted to escape.' There was a ripple of applause and modest smiles from the officers receiving this praise.

'Task Force Two, led by DI Jones from Dorset CID, also made an arrest. Again there were two suspects. One dived to his death through an upstairs window. The second attempted to evade arrest. We must thank Ken Jones for his bravery in tackling the second man, who was armed with a knife and fought ferociously. He is in hospital, under police guard, but is expected to recover from his injuries. I am recommending that DI Jones receives an award for outstanding bravery in carrying out this arrest.' Loud applause, led by a smiling Jenny.

From Ken, an embarrassed smile and a nod of recognition. The Chief raised his hand to quieten the audience and continued. 'It's clear that this is the work of an organised crime group with their fingers in multiple pies. The extreme lengths that the suspects took to avoid arrest, even prepared to take their own lives, fit this pattern. They know that they will be vulnerable to attack in prison – that their families in Europe will be in grave danger if the gang leaders believe that they will give evidence to the police that could incriminate them. This has been a great day for Hampshire and Dorset police. It represents an important milestone in our battle against major crime in our area. But the real culprits are still at large. We still have work to do. But for now, well done! Let's relax and enjoy the moment!'

21

As the small convoy drove back into Dorset, Jenny could see, by the set of his mouth, by the look in his eyes, that her boss was troubled. She waited until they were on a long straight stretch of the motorway before speaking. 'You did the right thing, boss. He had a knife. He would have used it if you hadn't tackled him.' Ken nodded glumly.

'Maybe. But I could have just restrained him and called for help. I really laid into him.'

'He was scum. Boss. He got what he deserved. You shouldn't waste a second feeling sorry for him.'

'I feel guilty…'

'About the commendation. I know. But no-one deserves it more than you. Don't look a gift horse in the mouth!'

'I hate them! I bloody hate them! Men who'll

treat women like that!'

'I know boss! And you're the better man for it!'

But Ken's face was still set in stone as they left the motorway and swung onto the A27. A long silence. And then Jenny tried to lighten the mood.

'What's the latest with you and your gorgeous pathologist lady! Surely she's come round to you by now!'

Ken laughed bitterly. 'He's moved in!'

'What?' Jenny didn't think she had heard correctly.

'He turned up at her door with a case and said his wife had turned him out. So she took him in. He's there now. Living with her.' He tried, unsuccessfully, to keep the bitterness out of his voice.

Jenny was still trying to come to terms with what she was hearing. 'You're joking me!'

'Afraid not.'

She stared at Ken. His chiselled features. His thick brown hair, with just the suggestion of a wave. A man she had so much respect for. It was incomprehensible. 'She can't be serious! He's almost bald. He's old enough to be her dad!' A slight exaggeration but keenly felt. 'He's an old man, for God's sake! And you…boss, there's no contest!'

'It seems there is. And he's the winner. Let's not talk about it, huh?'

Before she could respond, the phone rang. It went on loudspeaker. Nick, who had stayed behind at the office, had news. 'Boss? We've just got something back from forensics. On the charred papers. They managed to read the data from one. It's a bank statement boss. It shows a balance of over half a million. Regular payments of thousands every month. We've identified the bank from a bit of the name that was just readable. In the Channel Islands.'

'Good work, Nick. And is there a name?'

'No boss. But there was part of the account number. We contacted the bank. It's Carrington-Smithers!'

'Ah! So he's been milking the estate and pocketing a fortune! Nick – we're not coming straight back as we intended. I'm diverting the task force to Bishop Farthing!'

Jenny had a flash of insight. 'Alec — he was the estate's accountant, wasn't he? And he'd discovered something wasn't right! He could have sniffed Carrington-Smithers out, couldn't he? That would give us a motive. And he had access to all the guns…'

Ken nodded, his face grim, his hands so tight on the wheel that the knuckles showed white. 'He's in it up to his neck. Let's get him. He's got a lot of questions to answer! Nick — get an interview room ready. And see if he's got any previous!'

'Roger, boss. Oh — his Lordship's on his way, with the protection force. He'll be here in about an hour and a half.'

'Great news. If we're not back by then, keep him happy till we arrive.'

'Boss?'

'Plenty of tea. And whisky. Get a good bottle. Use petty cash!'

'Okay, boss, will do. Good luck!'

'Thanks, Nige, but we won't need it. This Carrington-Smithers is a posh arsed wimp! He'll be no trouble!'

Jenny smiled. Her thoughts exactly. Ken passed instructions to the van behind them. The klaxons went on. The small convoy raced at full speed towards the sleepy village of Bishop Farthing.

But Nick hadn't finished. 'Er — you might have more trouble than you're expecting, boss. You see, Carrington-Smithers doesn't exist.'

'What?'

'There's no record of him. Anywhere. He claimed he went to Eton. They've checked all their entry records. Never heard of him. He served in the armed forces. Only he didn't. No record of him anywhere.'

'So he's using an alias?'

'That or he's an alien visitor from outer space.'

'Let's hope not. Thanks, Nick. We'll bring him in anyway and see if we can identify him from fingerprints.'

As the small convoy pulled into the long drive leading to the manor, Ken had to swerve to avoid a jag racing in the opposite direction.

Jenny swung round. 'Was that him?'

'Couldn't tell. Too fast. Let's get to the manor and see if he's there – if not, we'll put a trace on the car.'

They stopped at the main gate. Ken rang the intercom bell. There was a frustrating delay. Jenny signalled to the officers in the van behind them to get ready to smash down the gate. 'Boss, shall I check the dashcam footage to get the number plate of the jag?'

'Good thinking, Jen. Put an alert out for it anyway, just in case.'

'Will do, boss.'

Finally, the intercom crackled into life. But it wasn't the butler who answered – it was a woman's voice. She sounded nervous and unsure. 'Yes?'

'Police. We need to enter these premises. Open the gate!'

'Oh. I'm not supposed to… I don't think I should…'

Jenny recognised the voice. 'It's the cook, isn't it? We met on my last visit. You spoke to me, DC Grace. You must open this gate and allow us in, on urgent police business!'

'It's not my job. I was told not to let anyone…'

'Open up immediately or we'll smash though the gates and you'll be arrested for…' There was a click and a whirr as the gates swung open. Ken and Jenny jumped back into the car and roared up to the front doors as the officers behind scrambled back into their van. Ken was impatient with manor houses, awkward servants, and locks. He thudded on the thick oak of the ancient entrance doors. Another frustrating delay. Finally, the sound of bolts scraping back and the doors opened.

The cook was wiping her hands nervously on her thick cotton apron, leaving streaks of raw pastry, long dirty cream scars, on the white fabric. Her face was flushed, perhaps from the heat of ovens, or from the stress of meeting police officers at the door. Her plump pink fingers were shaking. She tried to pull her black dress tighter round her rotund stomach as if it would protect her. Jenny tried to calm her, sensing that in her distressed state she would be of little use. 'Remember me? We talked last time I came here. You're not in any trouble. We need to see the butler: Carrington-Smithers?'

The cook looked slightly relieved but blubbered out, still flustered: 'He's not here. You missed him. Just missed him. He took one of the cars, I think. Couple of minutes ago…'

'Damn!' Ken snorted. 'He must have been in the jag that passed us! No point in wasting time here. You put out an alert for the car, didn't you?' Jenny nodded. 'We'll leave it to traffic to bring him in. He can't have gone far. Let's get back to base and see what his lordship has to say for himself. Let the others know!'

Obediently, Jenny walked over to the van and brought the rest of the small task force up to date, while Ken stared morosely over the grounds towards the bluebell wood, just visible, a line of trees keeping sentinel over the distant murder scene. He could not bring Elyse her husband back, but he hoped they were nearer to solving the mystery of his death. He could at least bring her some closure.

When they arrived back at the station car park, they saw the protection squad's car already in the space reserved for the Chief Constable. Ken steeled himself for a difficult interview –

273

knowing that top brass were going to be watching his every move. But this was for Elyse. She deserved answers.

As he walked into the office, all eyes turned on him. Nick and Geoff were smirking. 'He's in Interview Room One, boss. He's made himself at home!'

'Meaning?'

'You'll see!' they sniggered.

Ken passed two Royal Protection Officers, drinking coffee at the back of the office, who gave him a polite nod. Then he paused at the window to the interview room. An elderly but corpulent gentleman – obviously his lordship – was sitting with his feet up on the desk. On the table beside him was a Waitrose bag. Clustered round it was a variety of take away foodstuffs, most of them nibbled. A bottle of port stood beside this detritus, half empty, alongside a slightly grubby office tumbler. Another was in the gentleman's hand as he drank deeply, a happy smile on his face. Ken composed himself and entered.

'Morning old chap! Have a pew!' His lordship was in a surprisingly jovial mood. 'Help

yourself to the port! Bit of Tiffin left! Tuck in!
Have to say, old boy, the grub here is well below
par! Had to send out for some decent food! And
no alcohol on the premises apparently! Apart
from a disgusting bottle of cheap whisky! Poor
show, old man!'

Ken sat opposite him. 'We live somewhat
frugally, I'm afraid. Trying to keep costs down.
For the taxpayer.'

'Jolly good show, old boy! Completely
understood. Now, what can I do for you? Need
help with your enquiries – all I've been told. Not
a problem – as long as it doesn't take too long.
Like to be back at the old place in good time for
supper!'

Jenny appeared at the door, having stopped
at the loo. Ken sighed with relief and waved her
to join them. 'We'll be as brief as we can, your
lordship. I hope you don't mind. We need to
switch on the tape machine.'

'New-fangled devices! It was all note taking
in my day! Shorthand you know.'

'The tape machine is more reliable. No
chance of a mistake or misunderstanding.'

His lordship was magnanimous. 'Go ahead!

Not a problem! Glad to help!'

This was not the response that Ken expected. There was certainly no sign of guilt in this man. As Jenny settled down beside him, after giving him an amused glance, Ken decided to go straight for the jugular. 'The incident we're investigating happened three days ago. A body of a man was found on the edge of your estate. He'd been killed with a shotgun.' He paused, to observe the effect of this on the suspect.

His lordship looked totally amazed. 'Good God! Are you telling me they hadn't taken it away?'

'It's been removed now, sir. It's at the mortuary. One of our top pathologists has done a thorough post-mortem.' He studied his lordship's face, looking for signs of anxiety or guilt. There was none.

'Bloody bad show. Can't understand it. Shouldn't have left the corpse lying around for anyone to see. Rum do.'

Ken was confused. 'Just to clarify matters, sir, for the tape. You knew that the man was dead?'

'Of course!'

'And that he'd been shot. So who was expected to move the body?'

His lordship touched the side of his nose with his finger. 'Can't say. Hush hush. Need to know only. Only those who need to know!'

Ken leaned forward, determined. '<u>We</u> need to know, sir. Who did you think would hide the body?'

'If I tell you, son, I'd have to kill you! Official Secrets Act. Top level security clearance. Couldn't possibly!'

Ken was bewildered but decided to go back a step. 'We have the weapon, sir. It's one of your shotguns. We have witnesses who saw it in your possession on the morning of the killing. Your fingerprints are all over it.' (He was stretching things a bit here as they didn't yet have any prints on file, but he felt it was worth the risk.) 'So I must ask you, sir. Did you fire the shot that killed Alex Bartle?'

He expected a denial. He thought a momentary glimpse of guilt might cross his lordship's face. He checked the recorder was running and rested his hand on Jenny's arm to make sure that she was alert to whatever response this question produced, no matter how slight. The actual response, when it came, was the last that either of them expected.

'Bloody well did! Bloody good shot, as well! Straight through the heart! Would have hit him with the second as well if the bastard hadn't hit the deck so soon. Collapsed like a sack of drowned ferrets! Bloody inconsiderate!'

Ken and Jenny stared open mouthed, first at the killer and then at the whirring recorder that had chronicled this unexpected confession for posterity. He was just about to form a second question, when there was a tap at the door. It opened a fraction and Geoff whispered through it. 'Sir!'

Ken rose. 'Excuse me a moment.'

Geoff looked nervous. 'You've a visitor, sir.' He pointed through to the office. 'The Assistant Chief Constable!'

And there she stood, in full uniform, her watery eyes ice cold. 'I understand you have his lordship in for questioning, Jones?'

'Yes ma'am.'

'I shall be in attendance. In the capacity of

an observer. Bring me up to date.' Her manner was brusque. Ken didn't like the way this was going.

'He just confessed, ma'am!'

'Under pressure?'

'No, ma'am. Just came out with it. He doesn't seem worried. He was boasting about his excellent aim!'

The icy stare dropped another couple of degrees. At her desk in the main office, Gina stared at the coffee in her cup. It had been warm a few moments ago. In her imagination, there was now a film of ice on top. 'You haven't charged him with any offence?'

'It only just happened, ma'am. There's been no time…'

'Good. You're to do nothing. Nothing at all, you understand, without clearance from the highest authority!'

There was a limit to what Ken could accept. He had Elyse to think of, naturally, as well as natural justice. 'Ma'am, the status of the suspect shouldn't affect our treatment of him. If he's guilty, we should…'

'You'll do as you're told, Jones. This is a highly sensitive situation. It needs the most careful handling. You'll follow instructions. Or hand in your resignation.'

'Ma'am, I…'

'We'll go in, shall we? If you're still on the case, then follow me.' And with that she pushed past him and strode into the interview room, followed by a distraught Ken. She glanced at the clock on the recorder. 'A.C.C. Gribbins has entered the room at fourteen twelve hours to observe the interview between Acting D.I. Jones and his lordship. Good afternoon, your lordship. You may remember our last meeting. It was at the charity dinner in support of the Hinton Hounds.'

'By Jove, yes! Jolly decent claret, if I remember right.' He struggled to place her. If he had groped her that night this could be awkward. But as he assessed her chiselled features and flat chest, he decided that he probably hadn't.

'Chateau bottled from the old vines. 1956, if I remember correctly.'

He smiled appreciatively. 'Damned right!

You've got a nose, ma'am!'

Both Ken and Jenny stared at her, slightly confused. Yes, she did have a nose. Didn't everyone?

'I understand that there has been an unfortunate accident. A shooting in the wood near Bishop Farthing. A loss of life.'

'No accident! By God no! Superb shot, though I say so myself! Took the bastard out at eighty yards!'

She looked a little disconcerted. An anxious glance at the recording machine. It could always be rewound. 'If you don't mind me asking, why would you shoot at the man?'

He looked around as if there were ears everywhere. 'Not sure I can spill the beans, Alicia. All right if I call you Alicia?'

It wasn't, but she gave an accepting shrug. It was difficult to refuse. Jenny suppressed a giggle. Alicia!

The ACC resumed. 'I'm sure you had a good reason for what you did. Thieving? Trespass?'

'Shouldn't say, old girl. You need security clearance. Top level…'

'I can assure that I and all my staff are fully vetted. We are approved at all levels of security clearance.' This was news to Ken, but he kept his eyes on the suspect. Would he talk now?

'In that case, old girl, I'll reveal all!' His lordship visibly relaxed, believing that he could share the most secret information. Jenny stared at the ceiling in case he undid his trousers.

Alicia reached across Ken and, to his consternation, switched off the recorder. 'This is for our ears only, your lordship!'

He coughed appreciatively. 'I was told to take him out, old girl,' he whispered, conspiratorially.

She didn't blink. 'By whom?'

He leaned forward and, in a hoarse whisper, croaked, 'MI5.'

'You were under orders from the secret service?'

He leaned back and nodded.

'Who was your contact?'

He took a sip of port, pushed aside a plate holding a half devoured cream scone, and leered lecherously at her. The more port he drank, the more he fancied her. In fact, he had just discovered a weakness for women in uniform. 'They'd planted an agent in my home. For my protection.'

The Assistant Chief Constable picked up a pencil, expectantly. 'And that was?'

Things suddenly clicked into place for Ken. 'The butler!'

'Damn right! Amazing chap! Carrington-Smithers! I didn't twig myself until I told Snotty Snodgrass how pleased I was with him! You see, he'd given him one of the references. Turned out old Snodgrass had never heard of him. Never written a word about him. So I tackled the rascal. You've pulled a bit of a fast one, old boy, I told him. You said you worked for Snotty for years, but he denies all knowledge of you! What's going on, eh? Oh, he was a bit cagey at first. But then he came clean!' Another long sip of the port. 'The references were all a concoction of lies! Made up by Q back at base! Turns out he's an agent, put in to keep an eye on things!'

Ken realised his mouth was hanging open.

He closed it quickly. 'How can you be sure?'

'Went to Eton, old boy. No need to know anything else. Different house, of course. He said he was in Baldwin Bec. I was in Cotton Hall. Much better. We'd thrash them at rugger every day of the week. He had the same music master. Old Arky Snark! What a man! Need more like him! Make a mistake and he'd bend you over and thrash you without a by your leave! Cane never out of his paws! After a year with him I had an arse like beetroot, but good God I could play the recorder!'

Ken was quick to respond. 'We've done a search on him. Eton have never heard of him! What convinced you he was with MI5?'

'Simple, old boy! It was Smithers who found out about the Argie spy!'

'The what?' This was so ridiculous that Ken was tempted to end the discussion and charge him, but Alicia intervened.

'A spy? An Argentinian? What would he want?'

The elderly man slumped back in his chair, a smug smile on his face. 'Files! Documents! Artillery capability! Infantry tactics! Deployment round Port Stanley! Still got'em you see! In the safe! And this chap had been working with the maid. Getting her to slip them out of the house and down to the edge of the woods and hand them over! Honey trap! But Smithers spied her with her hand in the safe and followed her! Saw the whole thing! Tipped me off!'

Ken searched his memory. 'The Falklands War – it was in the early eighties!' He noted that his lordship did not look phased by the passing of thirty years. He probed further. 'Can I just check – do you know the current Prime Minister?'

A beam of delight crossed his lordship's ruddy face. 'Maggie of course! Wonderful woman! Best leader since Churchill! And what legs! A pair of stumps you could die for! Bet you wish you could bowl that maiden over, what old boy! If I still had the strength, by God I would!'

An attempt to bring the discussion back to reality. 'Mrs. Thatcher's been dead for a number of years. The Prime Minister now is Boris Johnson.'

His lordship almost rolled off his chair with laughter. 'Good God! You've got to be joking!'

'I'm afraid not, sir.'

'Old Bojo? Can't believe it! Couldn't run an egg and spoon race, let alone a country! Nice joke though, constable…'

Alicia intervened. 'Detective Inspector, your lordship – not a constable. We'll arrange for you to be taken home. I must ask you to stay on the premises for the time being. You've been very helpful to us. We may need to speak with you again.'

'No problem, old girl! And if you want to pop round for drink one night this week – you'll be more than welcome!'

Before she could reply, Ken, looking troubled, interrupted. 'Excuse me, ma'am. Could we have a word outside?'

'If you wish, Jones.' She rose briskly and walked to the door. Ken followed, leaving Jenny open mouthed, staring at their backs.

He came straight out with it. 'You can't let him go! Aren't we going to charge him?' His mind was spinning. He saw Elyse and her sister – all the people of the village, to whom they owed closure.

'With what?'

'Murder! Manslaughter!'

'Calm down, Jones. You've done well so far. Now is the time for mature reflection. He's a very wealthy and important man…'

He didn't allow her to finish he was so incensed. 'And that protects him – means he's beyond the law?'

'Calm down. Listen. He can afford the best lawyers. They'd have a field day on this and leave the police force and public prosecutors looking very, very foolish. He's clearly doolally. Certainly suffering from the onset of Alzheimer's. My own mother suffered so I'm an authority on the subject. If we try to bring a case, they'll claim he's unfit to plead and who are we to argue? If what anything he says is true, it's Carrington-Smithers you need to bring to justice. What's happened with him?' Ken looked blank. 'Find out, Jones. You're in danger of losing the plot!' And with that she waved to her driver and made for the exit.

Trish was sitting nearby, ostensibly staring hard at her computer, but actually listening carefully to all that passed between them. She smiled sadly and tried to comfort her boss. 'When I was a teacher, I came across women like that. Women who got into high positions – headships – just by sheer ruthlessness. Hard as nails. They think that because they're women they have to be harder than men. Don't let her get to you!'

'I know. You're right. It doesn't make me like her any more.'

'No boss. Shall I make some tea?'

It was traditionally the role of women detective constables to make tea for the team, produce sandwiches from thin air, go out for bacon butties. Ken was determined that this was not how it would be on his team. Everyone would take their turn. No assumptions about jobs for women. But this was not the time to make an issue of it. 'Thanks, Trish. You're a star.' He turned to Geoff. 'Any news yet on the butler?'

'Yes, boss. The copter has him driving north on the M3. Looks like he's heading for Heathrow or Gatwick. We've got cars on the slip roads ready to intercept!'

Ken was surprised. It seemed an age since

they had been standing at the door of the manor house in a frustrating conversation with the cook. He gave thanks for Dorset roads for slowing him down. In any other county, the suspect would be on a plane by now fleeing the country. 'When they pick him up, get him back here as soon as you can. He's our new suspect.'

'Roger, boss.'

Ken turned to the protection officers. 'His lordship is free to go. But he's to go to his home and mustn't leave there without prior permission from us!'

They shrugged non-committedly and strolled to the interview room to assist him to the car.

DI Ken Jones knew that he had to be ready for the man when they finally brought him in. He sat at his desk and chewed on the end of a pencil that was scarred with many past deliberations. They knew that Carrington-Smithers was not his real name. No-one in their right mind would believe he was a secret agent. He was a crook – possibly the master mind behind a criminal organisation profiting from prostitution, drugs, and forged merchandise. A multimillion-pound operation. But they needed a name to ensure they had the edge on him. He called the team together.

'Listen up, guys. Taken overall, the case is going well. Brilliant. Thanks to you all. Nick. Geoff, Trish, Gina – you've done great tracking down number plates, IDs, bank details – we couldn't have done without you. Jenny – some of your insights and tactful work with witnesses have been invaluable.' There was a quiet murmur of appreciation from everyone there. 'Just to bring you all up to date. It looks as if we have the shooter. He's confessed and we have it on tape.' This brought a subdued cheer from everyone except Jenny. 'But there's a complication. He maintains that he was tricked into it by the man we're tracking now. He's using the name Carrington-Smithers, but that seems to be an alias. When we get him in, I want to be sure we have all the info on him we can get.' Geoff's hand went up. 'Geoff?'

'News just in, boss. Surrey have picked him up. He pulled into Fleet Services and they nabbed him there.'

'Great news, thanks Geoff.'

'Thank God for toilet breaks, boss!'

'Right on. By the time he gets here I want to know who he really is and any previous that we can use against him. We need to be on the front foot. He's not going to be a push over. Nick – get over to the house in Bishop Farthing and pick up anything that might have his prints on it. Take prints from the cook, maid, any-one else around so that we can eliminate them.'

Nick jumped to his feet. 'Consider it done, boss!'

'Geoff – Jenny has dash cam footage of the getaway car. Get the best images you can of his face and put them through face recognition software to try to get a match.'

'Will do, boss!' The atmosphere in the room was electric - almost buzzing. Briefings had never felt like this under Longbottom, they all agreed. He never thanked them for the work they did. Always seemed slow so the meetings seemed to grind at the slow pace of his mind. Trish had once fallen asleep during a briefing and only a quick nudge from Geoff had saved her.

Jenny left immediately to get the footage

from the car and as the briefing finished, the incident room was alive with purposeful activity as the team focused on the task. It was clear they recognised that they were now working for someone who was on the ball and who also valued the contributions they were making. It made for a committed and motivated team. They liked Ken and it showed.

When Surrey finally arrived with the suspect he was complaining loudly – shouting and swearing his innocence. The more commotion he made, the more guilty he seemed. Ken signalled for him to be dumped in a secure interview room. Let him sweat. His team held all the cards. He could wait until they were ready – until the odds were firmly stacked in their favour.

Face recognition had come up with three possible matches. The dash cam images had not been clear enough – light on the windscreen had masked some of the features. But the fingerprints had come up trumps. Carrington-Smithers, it turned out, was a well-known con artist. His real name was simply Smith. He had first come to the notice of the police as a teenager at school. Selling drugs in the playground. He got off with a warning. His teachers put in a good word for him. Said he was a promising student – a university candidate. A close shave – it might have worked as a warning. But he was cocky. Thought he was invulnerable.

Despite the confidence shown in him by his teachers, he missed out on higher education. He lacked motivation and hard work was too much trouble for him. Two years later he was arrested in Dorchester market, selling fake Gucci handbags and Chanel perfumes. Not a serious offence, but the magistrates put him away for three months because he refused to cooperate with the police. He wouldn't reveal his sources.

He'd gone undercover after that. Although it was suspected that he had his hand in many pies, he was clever. And now it was clear that, as a reward for his loyalty, he had moved up the ranks and become a key player in an organised crime gang.

And he was now tied up in a murder enquiry.

22

When Ken had all the facts he needed, neatly typed on separate sheets – a thick wad of incriminating evidence guaranteed to bring a criminal to his knees – he nodded to Jenny and they entered the interview room together.

The suspect jumped to his feet as they entered, his face livid with anger and feigned innocence. Why had he been dragged from his car? What had they done with it? Why had he – an innocent man – been brought here and left for over an hour in an interview room, without food or drink? 'I'll be reporting this! See if I don't!' The fake posh accent was gone, dissolved in the boiling heat of his fury.

Ken waited patiently until the tirade had run its course, saying nothing. When the man finally ran out of invectives, Ken said simply, 'Sit.'

He did.

'You're here to help us with our enquiries into three serious crimes. The murder of Alec Bartle in woodland outside Bishop Farthing. Profiting from the sale of drugs, prostitution, and fake merchandise. And finally the theft of significant funds from a lord of the realm.'

The suspect half rose, his eyes glancing this way and that as if seeking a way of escape. 'Don't try that on me! If you're accusing me of any of this, I demand a lawyer be present before I answer anything!'

Ken took his time to respond. He switched on the tape machine and sank into a chair. Jenny perched alongside him, the dossier in front of her, unopened. 'So, let me get this right.' Ken was smooth and calm. 'James Carl Carrington-Smithers is requesting the presence of a lawyer.'

'Damn right I am!'

'Which leaves us with a problem. Please excuse me for a moment. I'll need to check this out. I'll ask my colleague for a second opinion. This isn't something we'd want to get wrong. We take such requests extremely seriously.' He half turned so that he was facing his second in command. 'DC Grace?'

'Sir?'

'What do you think? Are we allowed to use taxpayers' money to appoint lawyers to represent non-existent clients?'

Jenny shook her head sadly. 'I'd say no, sir. Definitely not. It would be a scandalous waste of funds, paid for by hard working people.'

Ken spread his hands wide. 'Just as I thought. We simply cannot appoint lawyers for clients who don't exist!'

The man jumped to his feet. 'What are you trying on? Are you stupid or what? I'm here in front of you, aren't I? What more do you bloody want? Stop playing bloody stupid games and get a lawyer here – fast!' He finished with a note of triumph. He had all the confidence of a clever man who is heaping sarcasm on those far less intelligent than he.

'Sit down.' Ken shuffled through the impressive file of papers and spent what seemed like an age staring at one. 'Well, that's odd. You see we've checked for any reference to James Carl Carrington-Smithers and found' - a long few seconds of deafening silence - 'nothing. You were educated at Eton. But oddly they can find no record of you.' The man calling himself Smithers began to look uneasy. He was sweating. He ran a finger round inside his collar. 'And then there's your army record. An artillery regiment, yes? We've searched the military data base. Strangely enough, they've never heard of you. Dental records? National health number?'

The man who called himself Smithers suddenly began to smile, ingratiatingly. He leaned back in his chair as if prepared, suddenly, to be open and helpful. 'I can see there's no fooling you! I owe you an apology. You're a lot brighter than I realised! There's something I should have told you. I held back – I shouldn't have. Please ascribe it to my loyalty to my employer…' Suddenly his upper-class accent had returned. He was the head prefect, reporting to his headmaster on the transgressions of other boys in his dorm. He was the posh little boy whispering to his mater that he'd seen his sister kissing the gardener's lad in the shrubbery. 'You see, old boy, the relationship between a butler and his master is inviolate. It's similar to that between a Catholic priest and a parishioner. It is my role to protect him, not to condemn him.' He spread his hands. 'But I see now that I was wrong. In the case of such a serious crime, my first duty must be to justice, To the letter of the law. To those fine officers of the constabulary who work every day to keep us safe!'

Ken leaned back in his seat. 'So – you're going to tell us that his lordship fired the shot. That he killed Alec Bartle!'

'You already knew?' He sank like a deflated balloon and then sprang back into life. 'I can provide evidence! I was a witness! I put the gun away! It had been fired! Twice! It was still warm…' He hoped desperately that this offer would deflect attention from his true identity. He hoped in vain.

'Well, that's kind of you, sir. A kind offer indeed. It's good to see how public spirited you've suddenly become.' Ken picked another sheet of paper from the file and leaned forward so that he was uncomfortably close to the suspect. 'But quite unnecessary. His lordship was here only a couple of hours ago. He has made a complete confession.' He waved the sheet of closely typed paper in the man's face. He was ashen now, beads of sweat breaking out on his forehead, his eyes glancing this way as if searching for an escape. 'But there is something you can help us with.'

'There is?'

'A motive. Why would he kill the estate's accountant in cold blood?'

'Ah!' He saw a glimmer of hope. A sudden surge of confidence. 'I can help you there! You see, he should never have had the guns! He wasn't fit! Probably thought the man was trespassing! Gung ho! I should have done something sooner! I just hoped, I suppose, that the worse would never happen! But I was wrong! I was wrong! I'll have to live with this for the rest of my life! That poor man! I knew him, you know! Fine chap!' He was trying, unsuccessfully, to force crocodile tears from his eyes.

'Trespassing? I don't think so. We have sworn testimony from his lordship that you tricked him into shooting the victim by masquerading as an MI5 agent.'

The man's eyes blinked in panic for a split second and then the familiar bluster kicked in. 'Really? My God! You can't be taking that seriously! The man isn't right in the head! He doesn't know his own bloody name half the time!'

Ken leaned back and smiled, more confidently than he actually felt. 'We'll see in court who's believed. A peer of the realm who sometimes forgets his name against a crook and fraudster whose name doesn't exist!'

The man sank back, his hands fluttering anxiously. 'I'll give you my bleeding name! I want a lawyer!'

'And that name is?'

'It's Smith. Carl Smith.'

Ken pulled another sheet from the file, like a conjurer pulling a rabbit from a hat. 'The same Carl Smith with previous?' He made a show of studying the details listed on the paper. 'Arrested for selling drugs in a school playground? Arrested again for trading in fake luxury goods? That Carl Smith?'

'Bugger.'

'Well, that Carl Smith – I'm arresting you for conspiracy to murder, for defrauding the Farthing estate of over half a million pounds and for living on the earnings of criminal activity, including drugs, fake merchandise and prostitution. You don't need to say anything at this time, but anything you do say…'

He was interrupted by Carl Smith jumping to his feet. 'How did you… Where did you...? Shit!'

'I'm sorry to tell you that your efforts to destroy evidence turned out to be pointless. Our forensic team was able to decipher the papers that you tried to turn into ash.' He exaggerated slightly. 'We know every transaction. And the emails on the victim's computer show that he had sussed you out. He was asking awkward questions about huge sums of money that were missing from the estate accounts. You, and the rest of the organised crime group, needed him out of the way. And rather than tackling that yourselves, you tricked a vulnerable elderly man into doing it for you! There's enough to put you away for years.'

'Don't you threaten me! A good lawyer'll tie you lot up in knots! You'll not get another word out of me until…'

Two things happened almost simultaneously. Ken shot to his feet and grabbed Smith by his tie, Jenny reached over and switched off the tape machine. The detective twisted the knot hard and pulled the man half over the table towards them. Ken was much stronger than his opponent, who began to struggle for breath. His arms flailed round like an angry hen, but he couldn't get free. Spittle began to dribble from his mouth as Ken pulled his face closer. The man's face was turning purple as he struggled for breath.

Ken spoke slowly and calmly, but there was no mistaking the anger pent up inside him. 'Don't come that with me. Scum like you make me sick! Those girls you brought here with promises of a new start. You've scarred them for life. Youngsters who could have been your daughter or mine – raped and sexually abused. Sold for your filthy profit!'

The man was crying, sobs coming in gasps as he fought for breath. Ken threw him back into his seat. Words came out as a croak, 'I never touched them! That was nothing – nothing to do with me! I was just a bloody go-between!' He was panicking. It had seemed the perfect crime. The estate had provided them with the properties they needed; plenty of initial capital to get them started; and then a steady, and lucrative income. The accountant had stood in their way when he realised something was suspicious. But when he saw the maid with her hand in the safe and then followed her to a meeting with Alec, he had formulated the perfect plan. He tricked the old fool into believing that Alec had to be shot.

He was sure the crime couldn't be traced to him. The maid would keep her mouth shut. She was in too vulnerable a position to make any trouble. And if his lordship talked about the shooting, he would be thought to be raving. Two gang members would get rid of the body before anyone knew anything about it. Alec Bartle would simply have disappeared. But the man-now-known-as-Smith sat cursing slow Dorset roads, tractors, and horse riders that had delayed the arrival of his associates. And then the difficulty of finding both Bishop Farthing and the entrance to the wood. They had arrived too late. The police were already there. And this young detective was too smart by far.

Ken leaned forward and now-known-as-Smith cowered back. 'If you want to avoid spending the rest of your life behind bars, I strongly suggest you start talking.' The guilty man gulped and nodded dumbly. Unbidden, Jenny turned the tape back on. She spoke slowly and confidently. 'Let's start with names, shall we? If you weren't a ringleader in the organised crime syndicate – who was?' Smith gasped. He paled visibly. He had to give something, but he knew the crime bosses would wreak a terrible revenge if he gave too much away.

A knock on the door. It was Nick. 'The Chief, sir. He wants a word. On the phone in your office.' Ken looked back at Jenny. Smith was starting to talk. She was taking notes to back up the evidence on tape. He turned back to Nick. 'You'd better get him a lawyer. Pick one who'll understand what a bastard this one is and who'll be more helpful to us than to him!' Nick smiled and nodded.

'I know just the man, boss!'

'Good. Oh, and you might find it takes at least an hour to reach him. I think that's all Jen will need!'

He walked to his office and picked up the phone, feeling slightly anxious. Would this be another attempt to release a guilty prisoner? Letting his lordship go had gone against the grain. He wasn't prepared to let go of this one.

'Jones?' The Chief sounded affable enough.

'Sir?'

'I've heard good things from Alicia. You were quite right to release his lordship into protective custody. Had a word with the public prosecutor. We'd have had no chance of making any charge stick. He could afford the best defence barristers in the land and they'd have ridden roughshod over our case. It would have just finished up a major embarrassment for everyone. All round. Bad for his lordship. Bad for the force. Bad for the prosecution. Doubtful actually if it would even make it into court, the man's brain's so befuddled.'

Ken had one last dig. 'Disappointing though, sir. The case was just about solved.'

'Oh, it is solved! You've done well, Jones. It'll probably go down as accidental shooting. Regrettable but these things happen out in the country. Now this other fella you've brought in…'

'Carrington-Smithers, sir. But it turns out his real name is just Smith.'

'And just Smith could be the key to an organised crime network?'

'Yes, sir. But it seems he was also the cause of the shooting. He gave his lordship a cock and bull story about the victim being an Argentinian spy, believe it or not.'

'Don't waste too much time on that Jones. It would be his word against another in court. Concentrate on the criminal activity. If we can put the leaders behind bars, it will be a major coup for the force.'

'He's with DC Grace at this moment sir. I believe he's ready to talk.'

'Offer him protection. He'll need it if he spills the beans and it'll make it easier for you to get what we need. By the way, I've been giving thought to your rank. I intend to move you from acting to full inspector from this week. And your second in charge – I'll move her up to sergeant.'

'Thank you, sir. It's much appreciated. She deserves it.'

'You've got a future in front of you, Jones. I see you as Super in a very short time. I've heard good things about your team building and sharpness. Incidentally…' There was a short pause. Ken waited, slightly confused and not entirely happy with the way things were working out on the case. 'DI Longbottom. He's decided to commence his retirement a few weeks early.

We've let him go. He's leaving the area. Got a second home in Spain, apparently, near a golf course. You'll be assuming full leadership of the team. Something else I want you to think about. His departure leaves a vacancy in the lodge. It would be a great asset for you in the future. Gives you important contacts. Helps your career. If you're interested, I'll be happy to propose you for membership?'

'Sir…I…'

'Think it over, Jones. Take your time. The offer's there!'

'I will. Thank you, sir.'

'No problem. Keep up the good work!'

Ken put the phone down, deep in thought. The investigation seemed to be unravelling. The closer he got to the truth, the further he seemed to be from getting justice. How genuine were the comments that the Chief and his assistant had made? Did the prosecutors really believe that guilty verdicts would be impossible, or was there undue influence at work? Was there one law for the rich and another for the poor? He was uneasy. And this offer to induct him as a mason… Was it intended as a bribe to ensure that he went along with the strategy they were promoting – or was it a well-meaning attempt to further his career? His instinct was to reject it. Secret societies, little pinafores and funny handshakes were not his scene. He had always been suspicious of the influence that members of such groups had on each other. He determined not to rush any decision on this and to concentrate instead on now-known-as-Smith and find out how much Jenny had got from him.

The rest of the day was taken up with recording Smith's confession and contacting adjoining forces to alert them. The work of bringing in the suspects had to be carefully co-ordinated. The series of raids were kept secret until just before zero hour and carried out simultaneously to avoid any tip offs. But the ACC wanted her moment of glory.

The Assistant Chief Constable led the press briefing two days later to bring the media up to date with the on-going enquiry. She skirted around the killing, merely stating that the investigation was close to closure and that there was no reason for the good people of Dorset to feel insecure. There was no gunman prowling the county looking for victims. She went on quickly to their amazing success in closing down a major organised crime syndicate. A dozen arrests had been made. Millions of pounds worth of drugs and contraband had been seized. More than thirty illegal immigrants had been taken into custody and charged with being sex workers. They would certainly be deported. This gave the press – especially the more right-wing elements – plenty to go on and they rushed away to praise these successes, giving little thought to the somewhat vague assurances that were given concerning the murder investigation.

23

It was a full month before the body was released for burial. The Chief Constable had agreed that Ken and Jenny could attend the funeral. They were to represent the force and so it was required that they wore their full uniform. Both felt stiff and uncomfortable. As detectives, they were accustomed to dress more casually. In Ken's case, the uniform suited him. He was tall and firmly built. The cap gave him even greater height and the total effect was smart and dashing. Unfortunately for Jenny, the uniform was less flattering. The new stripes on her sleeves made her arms look plump and her lack of inches meant that she felt shapeless and podgy.

As they drove along winding Dorset lanes, ancient hedges flashing past, the verges left uncut to protect wildlife, they talked about the case. They had received assurances about the house arrest that his lordship was enduring. He was watched night and day and was not allowed out of the house alone. In part they sympathised. The man was clearly not responsible for his actions.

The pair were less happy about the outcome for Smith. He was in a safe house now, many miles from Dorset, and had a new identity. If he was to testify against the criminal masterminds who had run the organisation, he would need permanent protection and anonymity. They both thought that he was a devious and dangerous character who had got off lightly. Too lightly considering how deep his involvement had been.

Ken mused on the outcome to the case. How different real-life policing was from the that in fiction. It was the exploits of Morse and Vera, watched avidly as a teenager, that had inspired him to join up. For them, the chase seemed easier. And when they accosted the villain at the end of the programme with the evidence they had gathered, there was an immediate admission of guilt. No problems with clever lawyers or friends in high places. The story would always close with the villain being put away for years.

Everyone had congratulated him on the outcomes from this case, but he felt unsettled. All those girls who'd been duped and abused were being deported in shameful circumstances. No happy ending for them. No pity for their plight. And no closure for the victim's family.

He thought, ruefully, that he would have to always do his best to bring criminals to justice, but he might have to lower his expectations. Face up to the reality of a justice system in which the worst villains were considered innocent until their guilt was proven beyond doubt.

It was on this journey that Ken confessed to Jenny that the Chief Constable had offered to induct him into his lodge. Jenny laughed so much that she almost wet herself. The thought of her boss – the honest, intelligent, handsome man she so admired – becoming a performer in their pantomime ceremonies was just too ridiculous. He was much too tall to wear a tiny pinnie and as for carrying a tiny briefcase – he'd look like Boss Baby! Ken joined in the laughter, good naturedly. He had decided to turn down the offer. The only problem was how to do so without offending the chief.

He'd decided to play for time. He had

assured the Chief Constable that he was pleased at the offer, but pleaded that he wanted to get more experience, to show that he deserved the honour, before accepting. He reckoned it may have bought him a couple of years. By then, the chief himself might have retired.

The small carpark at the Church of St Egladine at the outer edge of Bishop Farthing was packed full. The school parking area opposite was also brimming with cars. They had to pull into a field entrance, snuggle the car up against the gate, and then take a five-minute walk back to the church. No-one had gone inside yet. Many of the villagers shook the two detectives' hands. They were touchingly grateful for the police efforts to solve the crime and keep them safe. Many of these were neighbours that either Ken or Jenny had interviewed during their initial enquiries.

Ken waved to a bunch of farmers, with ruddy complexions and suits that had been a good fit many years before. Their figures had expanded since and they looked in danger of bursting out of them like the Hulk. Two of them, Ken had visited recently. One had sheep taken, the other had lost some agricultural equipment. Both had signs on their property warning intruders that there was CCTV in place. Neither, having paid for the signs, had gone on to purchase any cameras. Ken had helped them to source the best equipment and was now visiting other farms to help them too. He was building good relationships. Talk was that he was a decent chap who knew what was what. Praise indeed – from Dorset farmers!

The hearse arrived, closely followed by a black car in which nestled Elyse, her sister and Alec's mother. Jones the undertaker walked ahead, in an immaculate dark suit, a top hat, and carrying a smart black umbrella like an officer's parade staff. The crowd hushed and the men doffed their caps in respect as the coffin was eased carefully from the hearse and carried gingerly up the winding path where some of the ancient gravestones, with indecipherable inscriptions, stood deferentially to attention. Others leaned at crazy angles like silent, sad old men leaning on walking sticks.

The six pall bearers manoeuvred their way through the iron gates in the porch and into the dim chill of the small church, parts dating back to the twelfth century. Faint beams of coloured light struggled through the stained glass and pencilled their way into the interior, as if trying out the route: tentative, uncertain that they were welcome on such a sad occasion. The ladies who took turns to supply flower arrangements for the services, held only on alternate weeks because the living had to be shared with two other parishes, had gone out of their way to make this a special occasion. Their gardens had been raided for as many blooms as they could spare to enliven the ancient building on this saddest of days.

The service was brief. Neither Alec nor Elyse had been churchgoers and so a simple ceremony was best. The large congregation (the vicar silently wished that the church was ever this full) sang the two hymns gamefully, if not tunefully. A friend of Alec gave a short address, with a few appropriate anecdotes. A recording was played of his favourite song, a Bob Dylan classic. The organ played as the coffin was carried down the nave and out to the grave that had been dug ready at the edge of the churchyard, in the shade of an ancient yew.

The vicar said the necessary words, reminding all that dust returns to dust. A handful of soil was thrown down and it rattled on the wooden lid. Everyone waited with bated breath to see if an answering knock would come from inside the box. Elyse, her sister, and Alec's mother threw single flowers into the grave. Slowly the congregation began to drift away, having paid their respects. Each in turn shook Elyse by the hand and offered their words of sympathy. It was, thought Jenny, a bit like a wedding ceremony in reverse.

Ken and Jenny waited until all the friends, relatives and neighbours had gone. Only then did they walk up to Elyse. Ken thought how lovely she looked, in a chic black dress, her dark hair tied back, a neat black fringe half concealing eyes made larger by her tears. He held out his hand, but to his surprise she embraced him, pressing herself against him. 'Thank you,' she whispered. 'Thank you for coming. For everything you've done.' Ken was moved, but he knew of many officers who had taken advantage of young women who were as vulnerable as Elyse was at this moment. He moved back slightly, took her hand and murmured that she'd no need to be grateful, it was nothing. 'If there is ever anything I can do for you, just let me know.' She smiled sadly and nodded.

He left Jenny to give her condolences and turned to walk down the winding path toward the car. There was a woman standing by the lych-gate. She was tall and elegant, in high heels that made her long, dark stockinged legs look particularly shapely. With a shock, he realised that it was Sheila. He had been concentrating so much on the ceremony that he had never noticed her in the congregation.

There was no way of avoiding her. As he reached her, she put her arms around him and kissed him on the cheek.

'Long time no see,' she breathed.

'Yes.'

'I was hoping you'd be here. I just wanted to say…'

'Yes?'

'Don't lose hope, hun. It's not working out with him. Give it another few weeks and I'll be rid. Then the coast will be clear for us!'

She took a couple of steps towards the carpark and then half turned, gave Ken a flirty wave and blew him a kiss. Ken watched her walk across the rough ground to her car. She tried to be elegant in her high heels but stumbled slightly on the cobbles. He had never before seen so clearly who she was.

He turned away to wait for Jenny. 'You cold, calculating, manipulative bitch,' he thought. 'You can wait in Hell for all I care.'

THE END

Read the back stories of the people of the village — including the story of Peter's courtship of Beth and the attack on Dennis by Annette during lockdown - in 'Bishop Farthing'.

And if you would like to follow the career of Ken Jones as he tries to root out crime in Dorset's fair county — watch out for further stories in the series!

Printed in Great Britain
by Amazon